PRAISE FOR
Madeleine Is Sleeping

"*Madeleine Is Sleeping* is, literally, a dream of a book: mysterious, funny, and startlingly beautiful."
—Michael Cunningham

"A hallucinogenic fairy tale that veers between the clinical clarity of hard fact and a surreal mysticism . . . Bynum's lush, poetic imagery is full of vivid, sensuous details one can almost smell, taste, and feel." —*The Boston Globe*

"A voice at once sensuous and humorous, mellifluous and matter-of-fact." —*The Washington Post Book World*

"Audacious in form and content . . . Like a dream, this novel fills the mind with tantalizing ambiguity, haunting images, and innocent longings that are slow to fade."
—*The Christian Science Monitor*

"An enchanting novel that appeals to the naughty, insolent child in each of us." —*USA Today*

"Boldly original . . . No one will close *Madeleine Is Sleeping* without rediscovering how profound—and profoundly strange—adolescence is." —*People*

Ms. Hempel Chronicles

Also by Sarah Shun-lien Bynum

Madeleine Is Sleeping

Ms. Hempel Chronicles

SARAH SHUN-LIEN BYNUM

HARCOURT, INC.
Orlando   Austin   New York   San Diego   London

Requests for permission to make copies of any part of the work should
be submitted online at www.harcourt.com/contact or mailed to the
following address: Permissions Department, Houghton Mifflin
Harcourt Publishing Company, 6277 Sea Harbor Drive, Orlando,
Florida 32887-6777.

www.HarcourtBooks.com

Library of Congress Cataloging-in-Publication Data
Bynum, Sarah Shun-lien.
Ms. Hempel chronicles: stories/Sarah Shun-lien Bynum.—1st ed.
p. cm.
1. Middle school teachers—Fiction.   2. Women teachers—Fiction.
3. Self-actualization (Psychology)—Fiction.   I. Title.
PS3602.Y58M74   2008
813'.6—dc22   2008008924
ISBN 978-0-15-101496-5

Text set in Bell MT Std
Designed by Linda Lockowitz

Printed in the United States of America
First edition
K J I H G F E D C B A

For Dana

Contents

Ms. Hempel Chronicles

Talent

MANY OF MS. HEMPEL'S STUDENTS were performing in the show that evening, but to her own secret disappointment, she would not be appearing. All around her, she was confronted with reminders of the event: during morning assembly, an announcement (three eighth-grade girls bobbed up and bawled, in unison: Tickets on sale at the door!); pink flyers slapped crookedly onto the walls; a note from a parent: Please excuse Louisa, rehearsals ran late, she will turn it in on Monday.

Adelaide Burr cornered Ms. Hempel during homeroom and described her costume. Adelaide was an avid appreciator of dance. Her first book report had celebrated in a collage (dismembered limbs; blue glitter) the life and contributions of Martha Graham, and her second, a dramatic monologue, was based on a bestseller written by a ballerina who had suffered through several disastrous affairs and then developed a serious cocaine habit. Adelaide seemed excited by the lurid possibilities. "Just imagine!" she said to Ms. Hempel, and clapped her hands rapturously against her thighs, as though her shorts had caught fire. The bodies of Ms. Hempel's students often did that: fly off in strange directions, seemingly of their own accord. Now Adelaide told her that she had choreographed a solo piece to Beethoven's Moonlight Sonata. Balancing *precariously*, she said, on a kitchen footstool, she had peeled the glow-in-the-dark stars off the ceiling above her bed. "I have incorporated them into my dance," she said mysteriously. She made Ms. Hempel promise that she would come.

The building hummed throughout the day: older girls came leaping down the stairs, fishnet stockings streaming behind them like pennants. Mr. Spiegelman, his yarmulke slightly askew, heaved the grand piano into the auditorium. From the bowels of the science wing, a trombone bleated out a solitary, echoing rendition of "Luck Be a Lady." When Ms. Hempel went into the bathroom, she saw pots of lip gloss perched along the edges of the sinks. The girls hadn't taken off their makeup since the run-through that morning, and all day their faces had squirmed self-consciously, their sticky black eyelashes batting, their shiny mouths twitching over their teeth. It was all new to them.

Before the show, Ms. Hempel groped around the bottom of her pocketbook and found a tube of lipstick she had left there long ago. The shade was a glamorous brown, and as she hid in the faculty lounge, crouching over her compact, she thought, *Narcissistic,* and then corrected herself. Vain was more accurate, although not a vocabulary word. Colorless was perhaps even more precise. She rubbed a finger vigorously over her teeth: there were parents waiting outside the auditorium, herded together like hungry and disconsolate cattle; she would have to smile at them as she walked past.

The program announced that Adelaide would be the first performer of the evening. Beneath her name was printed in italics: *I wish to thank my family and friends for believing in me.* She entered the stage in darkness; the phosphorescent stars, sprinkled over the stomach of her pink leotard, glowed weakly, as if on the verge of dying. Apparently most of the adhesive had remained on her bedroom ceiling, so Adelaide had secured the stars with Scotch tape, which caught the light from her parents' flash camera and made her glisten like an amphibian. She still had a little girl's potbelly; her breasts were only nubs. A blue spotlight followed her nervously about the stage, lurching forward whenever it seemed as if she might leap into the air, which she did often, as well as collapse, methodically, several times onto the floor. Throughout, she kept her eyes fixed on some beautiful scene in the distance that only she could see. But the dance remained, in some fundamental way, incoherent: it reminded Ms. Hempel of her music-appreciation class in third grade, when Dr. Nicolucci would turn up the volume on the record player, flick off the lights, tell the children to shut their eyes, and then order them, threateningly, to move about the room. Ms. Hempel hung on to the edge of her folding chair and tried to see Adelaide as lovely and silvery and ethereal, like a moonbeam or a sylvan nymph. She finally decided: Adelaide is lovely on the inside, and soon the rest of her will catch up. For she admired Adelaide, who could easily have been a pariah, with her walleye, and her manic ways, but on most days she willed her eyeball into place and commandeered a sort of following.

The next girls were in fact beautiful. The three ninth graders stood frozen on the stage in a staggered line, waiting for the tape to begin. They wore shiny athletic pants in shy pastel colors that swished when they started to move. On top, their little cotton camisoles showed the black straps of their bras. Ms. Hempel worried about her own bra; all day it had refused to stay put, with one strap sliding down her shoulder at ill-timed moments. She suddenly felt what a relief it was to be sitting in the darkness. As a teacher, she felt herself the object of ferocious scrutiny; kids missed nothing; they spent entire days looking at her. Ms. Hempel was always getting chalk dust in her hair or, less frequently, on the tips of her breasts when she would stretch up on her toes and write the homework assignment across the top of the blackboard. Some days it could be lovely, this attention; but it could be tiring as well, and she was glad for a moment to be there in the audience.

The girls jerked about the stage in abrupt, perfectly co-ordinated movements, their faces stiff with concentration. Occasionally a voice would call out from the audience, "Go Jane," and the girl would glance up and beam. The song was friendly and familiar; Ms. Hempel slowly realized that it was about a man whose penis became erect while dancing with someone he really liked. He sang, *Girl I know you felt it. Girl you know I can't help it*, and Ms. Hempel felt herself go rigid with alarm; she was caught, again, in an awkward position: still young enough to decipher the lyrics, yet old enough to feel that a certain degree of outrage was required of her. If only she were truly adult, so that the words were unintelligible, the volume unbearable. Then she couldn't be held responsible. The girl backup singer sighed, *Feel a little poke coming throoooouuugh on yooooouuuu*, and Ms. Hempel peeked at the rows of parents radiating out around her. They didn't seem to mind, or even notice. Their faces were puckered, as they usually were during school performances, trying to see their children as she had tried: graceful, gifted, well liked.

If parents *could* understand the words, would they find the song acceptable? Ms. Hempel was actively developing her sensitivity to the appropriate and inappropriate. She still had difficulty distinguishing between the two: was it appropriate for her to laugh when a kid farted in class? Was it appropriate for her to wear stretchy fabrics? Ms. Hempel was not, she knew, a very good teacher. She made easy plays at popularity: dismissing class a few minutes early on Friday afternoons; beginning each year by reading the Philip Larkin poem about how your parents fuck you up; pretending not to hear when the kids did cruel and accurate impressions of her colleagues. She bribed them with miniature chocolate bars. She extracted compliments from them. She promised herself that she would decorate her classroom with photographs of great women writers, but she never did.

She had also discovered by the middle of her second year that the work she assigned her students would come back to plague her, tenfold. And the less work she gave them, the less she had to do. She noticed that another middle school English teacher had stumbled upon a brilliant solution: debate. It had the air of intellectual rigor, but you never had to bring piles of it home with you to correct. You just listened carefully and pretended that you were writing copious and detailed notes in your grade book. But she soon learned that she had no stomach for eighth-grade debate. It required a lot of newspaper reading, which she didn't enjoy, and too often the students would make sweeping assertions about terrorists' knowledge of chemical weaponry or atrocities committed by the New York City police or illegal dumping of toxic waste in residential neighborhoods, which never sounded quite right to her, but she didn't feel sure enough to correct them. She found herself, during November's Debate Unit, in the midst of a deafening storm of misinformation, a great deal of it rather frightening and, she feared, damaging to her kids' sense of safety and well-being. So they returned to reading novels and poems, a territory across which she stalked with much greater confidence. The literature they read was often bleak and depressing, but it was fiction, and none of her kids needed to worry about getting stranded on a desert island or working as itinerant laborers on an isolated and soul-crushing ranch.

This was her policy: lots of pop quizzes, because she could correct them easily in front of the television, and because they made her kids feel always a little bit afraid. But pop quizzes were not without their own pleasures, which she knew with a certainty stemming from her own days as a student. Now, as teacher, she would glide into her classroom, the stack of photocopied pages still warm against her chest, and she would sing out to them, "I have a surprise for you!" The kids would groan together, like a Greek chorus, but they still cleared off their desks, tucked away their books, swiveled their pencils in their tiny plastic sharpeners with a resignation and an eagerness she recognized. Because what are quizzes? They are everything that is reassuring about school: a line for your name; ten questions; blank spaces; extra credit at the end.

There were of course those children who didn't thrive under such conditions. Who muttered at her, or who cried, or who wrote nothing except their names and a heavy dark *F* at the top of the page: the self-condemned. The boy now lugging a didgeridoo onto the stage had been one of those: Edward Ashe, former piano prodigy, who by eighth grade had settled into a catatonic state interrupted only by moments of silent, unrelieved terror whenever she approached his desk. He had the biggest eyes she had ever seen on a boy, and he would widen them, like a camera aperture on a gloomy day, to suggest innocence and surprise: We were supposed to read chapter two last night? So genuinely panicked, so unconvinced by his own excuses, Edward could excite only pity. Ms. Hempel would move away and put another zero beside his name in her blue grade book. She did not believe in humiliation, though some other teachers exercised it to remarkable effect; she did not believe in making children unhappy when so many already were.

Edward, for example; he loved Scott Joplin, and had even composed his own ragtime waltzes, a fact that Ms. Hempel found difficult to believe; her imagination was incapable of seeing Edward Ashe's hands bobbing above the keyboard, his body rocking back and forth on the bench. The Edward she knew moved with a languor that sometimes slowed into complete suspension. When the period ended and the other children bombarded themselves against the door, he would remain in his seat and blink placidly. He never touched the piano now. But he would occasionally become animated by an overwhelming desire to communicate: He entertained his homeroom by tucking the bottom of his T-shirt beneath his chin, inhaling enormous breaths and distending his belly until he appeared pregnant, his skin stretched into a luminous and flawless dome rising above his corduroys. He had also perfected another trick, which involved string coming out of his nose. The kids particularly loved this one, but Ms. Hempel could not bring herself to watch it. And once he learned that she, too, owned and cared for a Colombian red-tailed boa constrictor, he would sometimes startle her by asking, in the lunchroom, or coming out of the library: "So how's he doing?" It would take Ms. Hempel a moment to figure out which he Edward was referring to. "He's very well," she would say, finally. "He shed last night."

Edward could write beautifully. He told tales from the perspectives of his beloved animals: three tarantulas, a ball python, and a boa constrictor. His favorite protagonist was the female tarantula, named Jenny. *Night falls. She is awoken by a hungry ache inside her belly. She stretches out her furry legs and surveys the sand spreading out around her. Hurrah! A small rustling in the distance. A cricket, a nice cute cricket!* In another story, he described Jenny gazing sadly out the glass walls of her tank. She watches a common household spider, busily lowering itself from the back of an upholstered chair. She is astounded by and envious of its weightlessness, its gift of self-suspension. She deplores her own earthbound and cumbersome state. Retreating to the darkness of a rock, away from the unforgiving glare of the heat lamp, Jenny thinks, *I wish I were an acrobat, spinning in the air.* Edward added a footnote that read: *This story is unrealistic. Spiders have very poor eyesight. Jenny does not know that she lives inside a tank.*

But now: Look at him! And that was the miracle of it all, how some kids found a way to grow into themselves. Edward stood in the middle of the stage, a tenth grader: stately, handsome, serene, his mouth pressed up against a gigantic wooden tube, producing beautiful and otherworldly sounds. The kids in the audience began to stamp their approval. "Eeeeedddddd!" someone howled. She could see Edward struggling not to smile; the strange, long moan trembled for a moment. And Ms. Hempel suddenly remembered the gift he had given her on the last day of eighth grade: The box, delicately wrapped in violet tissue paper, had fluttered in her hands, a small, insistent tremor, and instantly she knew what he had offered her. Through the cardboard, through the tissue paper, she felt a murmuring. "Oh, Edward!" she cried, "A rat!" It was the most thoughtful present of that year; she fed it to Marquez after school.

My milky thigh curves up to meet my cheek. That was what he had written. The assignment? A Description of Me. And whenever she saw Edward, that epithet sprang immediately to mind. As he toted his didgeridoo off the stage, she imagined the gluteal muscles contracting beneath his jeans. Ms. Hempel wiggled in her seat; her tights were easing their way off her hips, and she longed to yank them back up. But there was Mr. Roth, his nubby jacket scratching against her arm, and there was Mrs. Pierpont, who would turn to her and grin conspiratorially whenever the kid onstage did something clumsy and childlike. Ms. Hempel's tights slid farther and farther.

The audience greeted the next performer with shrieks and whistles. It was Mr. Polidori, whom the yearbook had voted the sexiest teacher for three years in a row. This was especially impressive because he taught physics, which was generally considered an unsexy subject, and because he had a reputation for being an inflexible grader. But he wore large collars and shirts made out of synthetic fabrics; his glasses were small and quirky; he grew sideburns. And he also played guitar, a sleek black one, which he now settled into his lap. The shrieking continued. Mr. Polidori raised his eyebrows in mock surprise; he bent down to examine the tuning pegs.

Ms. Hempel did not think that she approved of him. Once, in the faculty lunchroom, he observed that Mr. Peele, their principal, resembled an enormous walking penis. Why become a teacher, she wondered, if you had difficulty with authority figures? Or maybe, it occurred to her, that's why you did become a teacher. Mr. Polidori went out of his way to test the rules: he wore jeans and Converse sneakers, sauntered in late to faculty meetings. He freely confessed to having cheated a number of times when he was still in high school. Many of her colleagues, in fact, had cheated. Whenever the issue of ethics arose, someone would inevitably ask, "Well, we've all done it, haven't we? Taken a peek at a neighbor's test? Copied a passage out of an encyclopedia? Borrowed an older brother's term paper?" But, no, Ms. Hempel had not. Even as a second or third grader, she'd had a keen awareness of intellectual property. Her sense of herself as a *thinker* would never have allowed her to pass off someone else's work as her own; from her first days at school, she felt the importance of her mental endeavors. Her father was the one who had impressed upon her that intellectual labor is the most essential, the most valuable kind of work.

That was what was so sad and difficult about teaching. Taking attendance, enforcing detention, making them love you, always seemed to come first. Often the period would end before any knowledge could be pursued, and as for her own commitment to intellectual inquiry? She was just too tired, most of the time. Mr. Polidori, despite his inappropriateness, stayed until six or seven at night, preparing labs and dreaming up new ways of demonstrating the laws of gravity and motion. By that hour she was sitting before the television, numbly shuffling through her piles of pop quizzes. And besides, he was not wrong about Mr. Peele: his height, his probity, his crest of springy hair.

Mr. Polidori played an introverted style of acoustic guitar with discordant tunings and dense flurries of fingerpicking. Ms. Hempel could feel the admiration in the audience radiating toward him, the girls' delight at discovering that beneath his sometimes caustic exterior, Mr. Polidori was an accomplished and sensitive musician. And Ms. Hempel admired him as well; he was up there on the stage, and she was sitting on a folding chair in the darkened auditorium.

Dear Cilla Mitsui, who rubbed antibacterial gel on her hands at the beginning and end of every class, had asked that morning, "Why aren't you performing, Ms. Hempel?" Ms. Hempel was copying a list of transitional adverbs onto the chalkboard. "Me?" she said. "Oh, I couldn't, Cilla! I no longer have any talents!" And it was true. This time, she wasn't casting about for compliments. That is what is marvelous about school, she realized: when you are in school, your talents are without number, and your promise is boundless. You ace a math test: you will one day work for NASA. The choir director asks you to sing a solo at the holiday concert: you are the next Mariah Carey. You score a goal, you win a poetry contest, you act in a play. And you are everything at once: actor, astronomer, gymnast, star. But at a certain point, you begin to feel your talents dropping away, like feathers from a molting bird. Cello lessons conflict with soccer practice. There aren't enough spots on the debating team. Calculus remains elusive. Until one day you realize that you cannot think of a single thing you are wonderful at. "You have talents," Cilla Mitsui protested, and then paused, considering. "You are an *affable* teacher!"

Ms. Hempel was moved, but knew that *affable*, although a vocabulary word, was not synonymous with *good*. She was not a good teacher, yet teaching had rendered her unfit for everything else: She was not a good friend (she didn't return phone calls), nor a good lover (a student's smiling face would suddenly materialize before her, mid-coitus), nor a good citizen (she didn't have time to read up on the propositions before she went to vote). She had chosen teaching because it seemed to offer both tremendous opportunities for leisure and the satisfaction of doing something generous and worthwhile. Too late she realized her mistake; teaching had invaded her like a mild but inexorable infection; her students now inhabited her dreams, her privacy, her language. She found herself speaking as they did; anything cheap or worn or disappointing was *ghetto*: I'm so sick of this ghetto answering machine! she would exclaim to her empty apartment. Anything extreme was *mad*: The food here is mad expensive! she would say, examining a menu. *No doubt* she used liberally to indicate her emphatic agreement. Her one comfort was the mutuality of the exchange, for they, without realizing it, had adopted her mannerisms as well. Once she overheard Michael Reggiani refer fondly to Julius Levy-Cohen as irredeemable. Or when Kia Brown was sent back to the end of the lunch line, she said, I'm so cross! But really, victory was theirs; they had taken the castle and hung their flag from the turret; they had corrupted even her impeccable spelling. Ms. Hempel, crowned Grammar Queen of her junior high, now found herself confusing *there* and *their*, and inserting apostrophes where they didn't belong. It was a war of attrition; even the most egregious mistakes, seen over and over again, can begin to assume the appearance of correctness.

She put *e* before *i*. She bought blue nail polish; she felt tenderly toward the same boys whom her girls singled out as crush-worthy. Earlier that day, during after-school detention, Jonathan Hamish had reached out and grabbed her hand. She was teasing him; he wanted to make her stop. Briefly, stickily, his fingers closed over hers, and her heart jumped.

She had given him and Theo McKibben detention because they had traded punches during class; affectionate punches, not malicious ones, but she had already warned them. So she said, amiably, as she always did, "I'll see you guys after school." But it turned out that Jonathan and Theo were in far deeper trouble; only the day before they had had an encounter with the police. Joined by some other unmanageable boys, they had harassed the pizza-parlor owner on Seventh Avenue, rattling his garbage cans and pressing their faces against his windows. It was an act of vengeance; he had banished them after they'd showered a booth with Parmesan cheese. But he telephoned the police, and when the cruiser pulled up to the curb, the boys had already fled, with the exception of Theo, who was trusting and moonfaced and slow.

"Is this true what I hear?" Ms. Hempel asked when the boys showed up to serve their detention, and at first reluctantly, then with increasing gusto, they told her the story, interrupting themselves to insist upon their blamelessness: "We just spilled a little cheese—" "Maybe I bumped into one of the trash cans on the way out—" "Everybody knows that he hates kids—" And they looked so earnest, so indignant, that she couldn't help but tease them. Ms. Hempel frowned; she pursed her eyebrows; she rolled her eyes. "Sure, sure," she said. "Wrongfully accused. The two of you would never *dream* of doing something like that." It was at that moment Jonathan's hand shot out and landed upon her own, resting on the desk. "It's true!" he said, and immediately it disappeared again; the protestations continued. He thought nothing of it, she was sure; it was just another one of those bodily convulsions she so often witnessed—an impulse, a thoughtless intimacy, as when her students, lost in concentration during a test, confused by a question, needing help, would raise their hands and ask her, "Mom?"

Jonathan Hamish was not at the talent show; he wouldn't be caught dead. He was the toughest, craziest kid in the eighth grade. He would have been expelled already if his mother hadn't been the French teacher, with dark rings beneath her beautiful eyes and fluffy hair pinned up with a pencil. Ms. Hempel knew a lot about Jonathan even before he became one of her students: his unpredictable violence, his cruelty to the weak and maladjusted. "You can see it in his eyes," said Mr. Radovich, the sixth-grade math teacher. "He's not the same as other bad kids." Jonathan's eyes were pale blue, with the same charcoal smudges beneath them: he had difficulty sleeping at night and would gallop up and down the apartment hall-ways, slapping his palms against the walls. His father played the romantic leads in Noel Coward comedies and was gay. According to his mother, Jonathan was terrified lest anyone should know; he played four different sports and said faggot regularly. But he loved his father and would run up to him proudly, and shyly, whenever Mr. Hamish found time to sit in the bleachers and watch his games.

Jonathan took two different medications three times a day. It was easy to tell when he had missed a dose. His eyes would glitter; he would tip his chair until the front legs rose six inches into the air; his pencil would erupt out of his hand. Ms. Hempel learned that unless she kept him busy at all times, he would needle his neighbors, shout out Homer Simpson impressions, eat sugar packets stolen from the lunchroom, fall back in his chair and crack his skull open. So her questions were frequently directed at him, and she always gave him parts to read in class. It was unfair, she knew; she saw the hands frantically quivering in the air, the look of consti-pation on her students' faces. But they understood, and she loved them for it. They confirmed her hunch that children, despite their reputation to the contrary, had great powers of sympathy.

Powers that Jonathan, too, possessed. His heart went out to the characters in the books they read. He loved Lennie, the lumbering and deadly giant, and would flare up when-ever a classmate referred to the character as retarded. He also loved Mercutio. "He's a wiseass, but he's a good friend," Jona-than said, and when they watched the movie, he murmured, "Mercutio's the *man*." He had no patience, however, for Holden Caulfield. "He's just a mess," Jonathan said. "I'm sick of him

messing up everything he does. He needs to get his act together." Jonathan's disgust was such that he made it difficult
to continue the discussion. He snorted and interrupted: "He's
a loser! When are we going to be done talking about this stupid book and this stupid guy?" Ms. Hempel was surprised; she
had hoped Jonathan would like Holden, might see in him a
kindred spirit. How stupid, she realized later, bent over in the
faculty bathroom, sobbing, the faucet turned as far as it could
go: that is precisely the reason he hates Holden Caulfield.

All the girls loved Jonathan Hamish. They sidled up to
Ms. Hempel and whispered, "You know his dad's gay, right?
It's so sad; he can't deal with it." Even at the age of thirteen,
they gravitated, these tenderhearted vultures, to the tortured,
the afflicted, the misbehaved. They circled around him, wary
but ravenous, each hoping that she would be the one who
could render him gentle, that he would nuzzle softly in her
palm. He was compelling to them in a way that the class jok-
ers and malcontents and spastics could never be; he was bad
in some permanent and profound way. What set him apart
was his shame; he took no pleasure in his bad behavior. When
his classmates gleefully recounted his misdeeds—Jonathan
chucked a blueberry bagel at Mr. Kenney's head! Jonathan got
sent out of theater class for the sixteenth week in a row!—he
would retract into himself, refusing to look at Ms. Hempel,
his face darkening. He never felt the triumph that the other
kids believed was his due. Instead, Jonathan seemed wearied
by his bad behavior; the struggle that took place within him
was daily and exhausting: she could see it, wracking his slight
frame, leaving those ashy moons beneath his eyes. Some days
he would grip the edge of his desk, his knuckles blanching, as
if a fierce and implacable storm were threatening to tear him

away. Ms. Hempel found herself touching his shoulder during class for fear of losing him, and in the hope that the weight of her hand might somehow serve as anchor.

But he was not here now. Ms. Hempel's eyes combed through the rows of faces, though she knew she would not find him.

Harriet now took the stage. Her cape wafted behind her as she guided her little card table into the spotlight. Harriet Reznik, precious artifact of another age! Her thick, swingy helmet of hair, the bangs that looked as if they had been cut with the help of a ruler. Her clanging lunch box. Her indifference to television. Her adventure books, whose child heroes discovered buried treasure and tumbled down waterfalls and toppled tyrannical governments. Her stories of Christmases in Canada, the tangerine peels burning in the fireplace, the giant footprints she left in the field: an experiment with a pair of ancient snowshoes. Her cousin Wilfred, with whom she made trouble and renovated a tree house and took swimming lessons in a very cold lake. Her guinea pigs, her magic tricks. She filled Ms. Hempel with wonder.

Harriet shrugged back the satin folds of her cape and plucked from the front pocket of her jeans a coin, which she held up for the audience to see: "Here before you now is a quarter. A regular, normal, twenty-five-cent quarter." Ms. Hempel smiled; Harriet Reznik—exuberant soul, mischief maker, jumper up and down—did not like speaking in front of crowds. She kept her eyes fastened on the quarter; she spoke in the breathless, uninflected rush of small children reciting poetry. "Before your very eyes, I will make this quarter disappear." She waved the coin mechanically above her head, as if spraying a room with insect repellent. "Disappear into thin air," she repeated, and gulped. Her wrist flicked; her hand curled into itself; the cape shivered. Then, miraculously, the coin was gone. Blinking rapidly, Harriet held her palm out for the audience to examine: "Behold! No more quarter." She checked her hand as if she did not quite believe it herself, and for the first time she smiled. "No quarter!" She patted the air with her outstretched palm, and the audience clapped. A claque of girls in the front row shrilled. "Now, watch closely." And Harriet Reznik tightened her fingers into a tube, pressing them against her eye like a telescope. "Empty?" She presented the spy hole for the audience to peer through. "Nothing in there?" She righted her fist, so that the telescope transformed back into her hand, gripping a fat bouquet of invisible flowers. With the unemployed hand she dipped into the fist, from which she extracted, in a single fluid gesture, a length of red silk. It floated in her fingers. "Magic," Harriet Reznik said.

"I bet she's going to be gay when she grows up," Mimi Swartz, the head of the art department, had once predicted. Mimi was gay, too. And Harriet certainly was different from all the other girls in the seventh grade; she was without fear, utterly uninterested in the opposite sex, never betrayed even the smallest flicker of self-consciousness. She fancied herself an incorrigible troublemaker. Ms. Hempel went to great lengths to encourage her in this role: "Harriet Reznik, why do you plague me so?" she would exclaim, rolling her eyes up toward the heavens. Harriet liked to dart into Ms. Hempel's office during recess and distract her from her grading. "Harriet Reznik, you are the bane of my existence!" Ms. Hempel would say, and Harriet would cackle delightedly. She had a battery of pranks—finger traps, squirt rings, fake rattlesnake eggs—all of which she practiced upon Ms. Hempel. "Want some gum, Ms. Hempel?" she'd coo, offering a piece encased in a suspiciously generic wrapper. Her teacher would reach out her hand, allow it to hover over the stick of gum, and then, after a moment had passed, plant both fists on her hips: "Are you crazy? I know the way that mind of yours works!" Ms. Hempel would exhale, as if she had just had a close call. "Harriet Reznik," she would say, eyes narrowing. "I wouldn't trust you as far as I could throw you."

But she didn't like to think of Harriet Reznik being gay. Not because she had any misgivings about gayness; she just didn't like to think of Harriet becoming a grown-up. A selfish, terrible part of her didn't want to see any of her kids get bigger. Yes, she wanted to see Adelaide emerge from the wings, as luminous as a moonbeam. Yes, she wanted Jonathan to sleep well; she wanted Edward Ashe to travel the world, blowing on his didgeridoo, adopting rare reptiles and spiders wherever he went. She wanted to see Harriet Reznik make whole elephants disappear. But Ms. Hempel couldn't bear to think of them not being exactly as they were now, as she knew them. She wanted them to stay in middle school forever.

Ms. Hempel had once believed, foolishly, that teachers liked to watch their students grow up. She had written letters to the teachers she loved most, to tell them of her progress, her becoming. Upon graduating from college, she had even telephoned Mr. Mellis, who had taught her creative-writing class in the eleventh grade. "I'm going to be a teacher, too!" she announced breathlessly over the phone. She waited for his ecstatic reply. The silence hissed over the long-distance connection. "Well," he said, finally. "If you ever had a novel in you, Beatrice, it's certainly not going to come out now." And now she sat here, in her brown lipstick, on a folding chair, and wondered: would she ever write a novel, or sing in a band, or foment a revolution?

A volunteer hoisted himself up onto the stage. He was a father, but one whom Ms. Hempel didn't recognize. Tall and homely, he stooped down, as if longing to be the same compact size as Harriet Reznik, but she shot him a forbidding look and fanned the cards brusquely in his face. "Pick a card, any card," she commanded. The father danced his hand over the splayed cards Harriet held before him. "Do *not*, at any cost, show me the card you have chosen," she said. He extracted a card from the fan and held it to his chest. "Study your card. Memorize it." He did as she told him. "Once you are absolutely *sure* you have memorized the card, you may show it to the audience." The father shielded his eyes and slowly rotated his outstretched arm from one side of the auditorium to the other, displaying his selection. Parents, kids, teachers, all leaned forward at once. A six of spades. Ms. Hempel heard a little boy somewhere behind her whisper it to himself. "You may replace the card," Harriet Reznik said. Frowning deeply, she shuffled the deck, cut it, stirred the cards around on her little card table. Then, abruptly, she swept them into a pile and rapped them against the heel of her palm. After placing the deck in the center of her table, she waited, face straining; she seemed to count silently to ten. The magic book's instructions must have included, Ms. Hempel realized, this moment of suspense. Now Harriet Reznik was ready to continue. "Is this," she asked, delicately tweezing a card off the top of the pile, "your card?" With an uncharacteristic flourish, she snapped back her cape. The audience gasped. The father's mouth opened and closed.

It was not his card. The card that Harriet Reznik held before her was not the six of spades; it was the eight of diamonds.

The father paused. Lie! Just lie! Ms. Hempel willed him to do it: Lying won't kill you. But then, with terrible reluctance, he shook his head. Harriet Reznik looked stunned; she flipped over the card, stared at it; she peered closely at the father: "Are you sure?" She asked it very politely. Ms. Hempel, sitting on her plastic chair, wanted to be someplace far away, and to take Harriet Reznik, cape trailing, along with her. She folded her program into smaller and smaller squares. The father looked searchingly into the wings, as if hoping some benevolent figure offstage might come out and rescue him. Harriet, with painful concentration, returned the wrong card to the top of the pile. "You can sit down now," she said.

The father walked out to the edge of the stage and bent down so that he could ease himself off. He seemed anxious to return to his seat, to the child waiting for him there. "Hold on!" Harriet Reznik shouted. The audience sat up; the man stopped, mid-crouch. "Wait!" she cried. "What's sticking out of your back pocket?" The father straightened, bewildered, and turned to face her. As he did so, Ms. Hempel saw that Harriet was right: there was something square, and stiff, protruding from his rear pocket. "Is that one of my cards?" Harriet asked. It was. The six of spades.

The entire auditorium shuddered. "Oh god!" the little boy said, involuntarily. "Oh god! Oh god!" The applause was thunderous. Parents clutched at each other and hollered, utterly without embarrassment. Kids cupped their hands over their mouths and sounded long, keening cries. Up onstage, standing behind her card table, Harriet Reznik gleamed. "Just wait till you see the next one!" she shouted over the noise.

Suddenly there was a wild rustling. From beneath her little table, from inside a cardboard box punctured with holes, Harriet Reznik coaxed a bird: not a dove, or some other mild-mannered sort, but a glossy and muscular crow. It cawed loudly. It flapped its enormous wings. It tipped over its box, struggled out of Harriet's grip, and took flight. The audience inhaled, their heads craning as they followed its path around the auditorium, black wings beating the air. The crow swooped low; boys reached up to catch ahold of it; Mrs. Willoughby took shelter beneath her program; adults tucked the heads of small children under the crooks of their arms; Mr. Radovich barreled toward the emergency exit; Harriet Reznik stood onstage, mouth agape, marveling at what she had unleashed. Ms. Hempel watched it glide toward her—shiny feathers, hoarse call—and lifting up an arm, she stretched out her fingers: She touched it!

Accomplice

IT WASN'T EVEN HALLOWEEN YET, but Ms. Hempel was already thinking about her anecdotals. The word, with all its expectations of intimacy and specificity, bothered her: an adjective in the guise of a noun, an obfuscation of the fact that twice a year she had to produce eighty-two of these ineluctable *things*. Not reports, like those written by other teachers at other schools, but anecdotals: loving and detailed accounts of a student's progress, enlivened by descriptions of the child offering a piercing insight or aiding a struggling classmate or challenging authority. It was a terrible responsibility: to render, in a recognizable way, something as ineffable as another human being, particularly a young one. On average she would spend an hour writing about each child, and then waste up to another hour rereading what she had just written, in the hopes that her words might suddenly reveal themselves as judicious. But too often Ms. Hempel's anecdotals reminded her of those blurry portraits from photography's early days: is that a hand I see? A bird? The sitter has squirmed, readjusted her skirts, swatted at a fly: she is no longer a child, but a smudge of light. This is how Ms. Hempel's students appeared, captured in her anecdotals: bright and beautiful and indistinct.

The cubicle where she now sat, peeling an orange, would, in less than two months, become a Faculty Work Station. Other faculty members would sit in the work stations next to hers; they would peer over and say, "Don't kill yourself. You're not writing a novel." But now there was only Mr. Polidori, humming faintly and balancing equations.

The science and math teachers had it easy. During anecdotal season, Ms. Hempel would berate her younger, student self: she never should have turned away from the dark and gleaming surfaces of the lab. She had chosen instead the squishy embrace of the humanities, where nothing was quantifiable and absolute, and now she was paying for all those lovely, lazy years of sitting in circles and talking about novels. Mrs. Beasley, the head of the math department, had perfected an anecdotal formula: she entered the student's test scores, indicated whether his ability to divide fractions was "strong," "improving," or "a matter of concern," and then ended with either congratulations or exhortations, whichever seemed more appropriate. The formulaic would not do, however, for an English teacher. Ms. Hempel could not complain of a child's limited vocabulary or plodding sentences without putting on a literary fireworks display of her own. Because there was always that skepticism: students who didn't quite believe that she could do all the things that she required of them (vary your sentence structure—incorporate metaphors—analyze, not summarize!), as if she were a fleshy coach who relaxed on the bleachers while the team went panting around the gym.

So the anecdotals must be beautiful. But she didn't want them to sound florid, or excessive. She didn't want to sound insincere. (Oh, superlatives! Ms. Hempel's undoing.) She wanted to offer up tiny, exact, tender portraits of the children she taught, like those miniature paintings that Victorians would keep inside their lockets along with a wisp of hair. And though she would fail to do so every time, she had not resigned herself to failure, could not experience that relief; every December and every May she would sit down to write, dogged by the fear that she would misrepresent a child, or that through some grievous grammatical error, some malapropism, some slip, she would expose herself, that she would by her own hand reveal the hoax.

"If I started my anecdotals this afternoon, I would have to write only one and a half a day. That sounds manageable."

"Recycle," Mr. Polidori said from the depths of his cubicle.

"I do recycle," Ms. Hempel said. "I make my kids recycle, too."

Mr. Polidori's face appeared above her. "Use your anecdotals from last year. Just insert new names—if you go under Edit, then slide your arrow down to Replace, it's quite straightforward."

"Oh," she said. "I can't do it. Because the material is all new this year. They're not reading *A Light in the Forest* anymore. Or *April Morning*. But it's a wonderful idea." This possibility had never occurred to her.

For the new seventh-grade curriculum, Ms. Hempel picked a book that had many swear words in it. She felt an attraction to swear words, just as she did to cable television, for both had been forbidden in her youth. Her father had considered swear words objectionable on the grounds of their very ordinariness. "Everyone uses the same old expletives over and over again," he said. "And *you* are not everyone." He grasped her cranium gently in one hand and squeezed, as if testing a cantaloupe at the farmers market. "Utterly unordinary," he declared.

But to Ms. Hempel, swear words were beautiful precisely because they were ordinary, just as gum snapping and hair flipping were beautiful. She once longed to become a gum-snapping, foulmouthed person, a person who could describe every single thing as *fucking* and not even realize she was doing it.

In this, she never succeeded. When she read *This Boy's Life*, when she saw *shit* and even *fuck* on the page, she quietly thrilled. Then she ordered copies for the seventh grade.

"First impressions?" she asked, perched atop her desk, her legs swinging. "What do you think?"

The seventh graders looked at each other uneasily. They had read the opening chapter for homework. A few stroked the book's cover, of which they had already declared their approval; it was sleek and muted. Grown-up. A cover that promised they were venturing into new territory: no more shiny titles, endorsements from the American Library Association, oil paintings of teenagers squinting uncertainly into the distance.

"Do you like it?" Ms. Hempel tried again. She smiled entreatingly; her shoes banged against her desk. Teaching, she now understood, was a form of extortion; you were forever trying to extract from your students something they didn't want to part with: their attention, their labor, their trust.

David D'Sousa, ladies' man, came to her assistance. Even though he was a little chubby and overcurious about sex, he was a very popular boy in the seventh grade. He had gone out with a lot of girls. He walked down the hallways with the rolling, lopsided gait of the rappers he so fervently admired. In the classroom his poise deserted him; he sputtered a lot, rarely delivering coherent sentences. He batted away his ideas just as they were escaping from his mouth.

But David was a gentleman, ready to sacrifice his own dignity in order to rescue Ms. Hempel's. *Cooperative* and *responsive.* she thought. *Willing to take risks.*

"It's like . . . ," he began, and stopped. Ms. Hempel smiled at him, nodding furiously, as if pumping the gas pedal on a car that wouldn't start. "It's . . ." He grabbed his upper lip with his bottom teeth. He ground his palm into the desk. The other kids delicately averted their eyes; they concentrated on caressing the covers of their books. "It's . . . *different* from the other stuff I've read in school."

The class exhaled: yes, it was different. They spoke about it as if they didn't quite trust it, particularly the boys, as if there was something inherently suspicious about a book whose characters seemed real. Toby, for example—the narrator. He wanted to be a good kid, but couldn't stop getting into trouble; he loved his mother a lot, but wasn't above manipulating her into buying things that he wanted—it was all uncannily familiar. They were also puzzled by the everyday nature of his struggles: There was no sign that soon Toby would be surviving on his own in the wilderness, or traveling into the future to save the planet from nuclear disaster.

"It doesn't really sound like a book," said Emily Radinsky, capricious child, aspiring trapeze artist, lover of Marc Chagall. Ms. Hempel would write, *Gifted.*

"I normally don't like books," said Henry Woo, sad sack, hanger-on, misplacer of entire backpacks. Ms. Hempel would write, *Has difficulty concentrating.*

"It's okay for us to be reading this?" said Simon Grosse, who needed to ask permission for everything. Ms. Hempel would write, *Conscientious.*

———

ON PARENTS' NIGHT, MS. HEMPEL felt fluttery and damp. She knew from past experience that she would make a burlesque of herself, that her every sentence would end with an exclamation point, and her hands would fly about wildly and despairingly, like two bats trapped inside a bedroom. The previous year, a boy named Zachary Bouchet had reported, "My mother says that you smile too much."

In the faculty room, Mr. Polidori threw an arm around her and whispered, "Just pretend they're naked."

That was the last thing Ms. Hempel wanted to imagine.

Instead, she decided to picture her own parents sitting in front of her. She pictured her mother, who would make them late because she had misplaced the car keys; and her father, who would station himself in the front row and ask embarrassing questions. Embarrassing not in their nature, but embarrassing simply because he had asked them. Her father liked to attract attention. "*Ni hao ma!*" he would greet the waiters at the Chinese restaurant. "Yee-haw!" he would whoop at the fourth-grade square dance recital. "Where's the defense?" he would wail from the sidelines of soccer games. "Brava! Brava!" he would sing out, the first to rise to his feet. Ms. Hempel, as a child, had received several standing ovations, all induced by her beaming, cheering, inexorable father.

Each of these parents, Ms. Hempel told herself, is as mortifying as mine were.

A mother began: "This book they're reading—I was just wondering if anyone else was troubled by the language."

Ms. Hempel smiled bravely at the instigator. "I'm glad you brought that up," she said, and reminded herself: This woman can never find her car keys. This woman is always running late.

A classroom of parents, squeezed into the same chairs that their children occupied during the day, looked at Ms. Hempel. She couldn't say, Your kids are okay with me. I promise. Instead, she said, "When I chose this book, I was thinking of *The Catcher in the Rye*. Because every time I teach *Catcher* to the eighth grade, I feel like I'm witnessing the most astonishing thing. It's like they've stuck their finger in a socket and all their hair is standing on end. They're completely *electrified*. What they're responding to, I think, is the immediacy and authenticity of the narrator's voice. And part of what makes Holden sound authentic to them is the language he uses. This book's impact on them is just—*immeasurable*. Even the ones who don't like to read, who don't like English. It suddenly opens up to them all of literature's possibilities. Its power to speak to their experiences."

Ms. Hempel paused, surprised. She had recovered.

"I thought to myself, Shouldn't the seventh grade get the chance to feel that? That shock of recognition?"

And she meant it, in a way, now that she had to say it.

What happened then? Ms. Hempel doubted it had anything to do with her speech. Perhaps an insurgency had been building quietly against the concerned mother, who probably hijacked Parents Association meetings, or else was always suggesting another bake sale. Maybe they heard in her complaint an echo of their own parents, or they believed on principle that words could never be dirty. Maybe sitting in the plastic desk-chairs reminded them of what school felt like.

One after another, the parents began describing their children: She talks about it at dinner. He takes it with him into the bathroom. You don't understand—the last thing that she enjoyed reading was the PlayStation manual.

They spoke in wonder.

At nights, I hear him chuckling in his bedroom. He says that he wants me to read it, that he'll loan me his copy when he's done. When I offered to rent the movie for her, she said that she didn't want to ruin the book.

"I knew it!" a father announced. "It was just a question of finding the right book."

And the parents nodded again, as if they had always known it, too.

"Well done!" Another father, sitting in the back row, began to clap. He smiled at Ms. Hempel. Three more giddy parents joined in the applause.

Ms. Hempel, standing at the front of the classroom, wanted to bow. She wanted to throw a kiss. She wanted to say thank you. Thank you.

And then it occurred to her: perhaps what had so humiliated her about her father had made someone else—a square dancer, a waiter, the director of the seventh-grade production of *Cats*—feel wonderful.

THE NEXT MORNING, IN HOMEROOM, Ms. Hempel helped Cilla Matsui free herself from her crippling backpack. "Your dad," she noted, "has this very benevolent presence."

"Benevolent?" Cilla Matsui asked.

Ms. Hempel always used big words when she spoke; they also appeared frequently in her anecdotals, words like *acuity* and *perspicacious.* It was all part of her ambitious schemes for vocabulary expansion. Most kids took interest in new words only if they felt they had something personal at stake. "You're utterly depraved, Patrick," she would say. "No, I won't. Look it up. There's about six of them sitting in the library."

So Adelaide's comments were astute. Gloria had an agile mind. Rasheed's spelling was irreproachable. Even those who weren't academically inclined deserved a dazzling adjective. David D'Sousa, for instance, was chivalrous. These words, Ms. Hempel knew, were now permanently embedded. Even after the last layer of verbal detritus had settled, they would still be visible, winking brightly: yes, I *was* an iconoclastic thinker.

Because one never forgets a compliment. "You looked positively beatific during the exam," Miss Finch, her tenth-grade English teacher, had told her. "Staring out the window, a secret little smile on your face. I was worried, to tell the truth. But then you turned in the best of the bunch."

Thus, *beatific*—blissful, saintly, serenely happy—was forever and irrevocably hers. She shared the new word with her father; she showed him the grade she had received. Aha, he said, with great vindication. Aha!

Uncomplimentary words, however, seemed to overshadow the complimentary ones. That wasn't it, exactly. But whereas an ancient compliment would suddenly, unexpectedly, descend upon her, spinning down from the sky like a solitary cherry blossom, words of criticism were familiar and unmovable fixtures in the landscape: fire hydrants, chained trash cans, bulky public sculptures. They were useful, though, as landmarks. Remember? she used to say to her father: Mr. Ziegler. White hair. He made us memorize Milton. And when that failed, she would say: Don't you remember him? He was the one who called me lackadaisical.

Her mother's memory was terrible, but her father could always be counted on. In his neat, reliable way, he sorted and shelved all the slights she had endured. Oh yes, he'd say. *Mr. Ziegler.* Looking back on those conversations, she wondered if perhaps it wasn't fair to make him revisit the unhappy scene of her high school career. Remembering old criticisms is only fun once they have been proven laughably incorrect. Fractions! the famous mathematician hoots: Mrs. Beasley said I was hopeless at fractions!

When her father died, a year ago that spring, Ms. Hempel had spoken at his memorial service, along with her brother and their much younger sister. Calvin talked about a day they went hiking together in Maine, and Maggie, before she started crying, remembered how he used to read aloud to her every night at bedtime, something she still liked to do with him even though she was ten years old now and capable of reading *The Hobbit* on her own. Ms. Hempel's story sounded unsentimental by comparison. She described her father picking her up from play practice, when she was maybe fourteen or fifteen. It was winter, and too cold to wait for the bus. Before parking the car in the garage, he would deposit her at the back door, so that she wouldn't have to walk through the slush. As she balanced her way up the path, he would flick his headlights on and off. The beams cast shadows across the lawn, making everything seem bigger than it really was: the randy cat, her mother's beloved gazebo, the fur sprouting from the hood of her parka. At the moment she reached the door, she would turn around and wave at him. She couldn't see him, because the headlights were too bright, but she could hear him. Click, click. Click, click. Only once she stepped inside would he steer the car back out of the driveway.

When Ms. Hempel finished speaking, she looked out at her family. They looked back at her expectantly, waiting to hear the end of the story. The last time she stood on this pulpit, many years before, she had received the same anxious look. She was the narrator for the Christmas pageant, and though she had spoken her part clearly and with dramatic flair, she forgot to say her final line: "So the three wise men followed the star of Bethlehem." A long pause followed, and then the three wise men stumbled out of the sacristy, as if a great force had propelled them.

For the rest of the pageant, she had to stay inside the pulpit, from where she was supposed to look down on the manger with a mild and interested expression; instead, she watched the other children wolfishly, willing someone else to make a mistake more terrible than her own. No one did. It could have happened to anyone, her mother would tell her, but she knew differently: it could have happened only to her. During her narration, she had fastened her eyes on the choir loft, but as she neared the end, in anticipation of the delicious relief that she would soon feel, she allowed her gaze to slip down onto the congregation below. There she saw her father, leaning forward very slightly, and holding on to the pew in front of him. He was smiling at her. Hugely. She lost her bearings entirely.

Now, standing in the same pulpit, she looked out at her family as they waited hopefully for a final paragraph. She looked at them in defiance: That's all! He clicked the headlights on and off. The End. And she wished something that she never used to wish: that her father was there, on the edge of his pew. He would have liked the story; it would have made sense to him.

"Is being benevolent a good thing or a bad thing?" Cilla Matsui asked.

"A good thing!" said Ms. Hempel. "Benevolent means 'generous and kind.'"

"Oh yes," Cilla said. "That sounds like my dad."

DWIGHT, TOBY'S STEPFATHER, was the character in the book whom her kids despised most. They shuddered at the humiliations that he made Toby endure: shucking whole boxes full of foul-smelling horse chestnuts, attending Boy Scouts in a secondhand uniform, playing basketball in street shoes because he wouldn't fork out the money for sneakers. They hated him for coming between Toby and his mother. They hated him for being petty and insecure and cruel. "Dwight . . . ," they would mutter helplessly. "I want to kill the guy."

As Toby's situation worsened, they would turn over their books and study the author's photograph: his handsome, bushy mustache, his gentle eyes. "He teaches at Syracuse," they would point out. "He lives with his family in upstate New York."

They loved these facts, because reading about the abusive stepdad, the failures at school, the yearnings to escape, to be someone else—it made them feel terrible. "He had such a tough life," they repeated, shaking their heads. "A really tough life."

But, according to the back of the book, Toby prevailed. The kids saw, in the felicitous pairing of picture and blurb, a happy ending to his story: he became a writer! He didn't turn into a drunk or a bum. The back cover promised that it was possible to weather unhappy childhoods, that it was possible to do lots of bad things and have lots of bad things done to you—and the damage would not be irreparable. Often a particularly somber discussion of Toby's struggles would conclude with this comforting thought: "And now he's a famous and successful writer." *Tobias Wolff.*

Fame and success: did that count as revenge? The seventh grade had a lively sense of justice. They wanted to see Dwight pay for all that he had done to Toby and his mother, for all the pain he had inflicted. They longed for a climactic, preferably violent, showdown between the boy and the stepfather. Barring that, they wanted Dwight to suffer in some specific and

prolonged way. The fact that he had to live with the meager-
ness of his own soul—this was not considered punishment
enough.

"He's probably read the book, right?" Will Bean asked.

"And he knows that Toby's a famous writer?"

They relished this idea: Dwight as an unrepentant old
man, hobbling down to the liquor mart, pausing by the brilliant window of a bookstore. And there's Toby. Mustached,
mischievous Toby, the same photograph from the back cover,
only much larger. A careful pyramid of his books is pointing toward the sky. NUMBER ONE BESTSELLER, the sign reads.
Through the plate glass, the old man can hear the faint slam-
ming of the cash register. He can see the customers taking
their place in line. And he can make out, even though his eyes
are old and rheumy, the title of the book that they hold in their
hands.

"If he's read it, he knows that millions of people now hate
him, right?"

Which would mean, of course, banishment from the Elks
Club. Divorce papers from his latest wife. Bushels of hate mail
thumping against his screen door. Furtive trips to the conve-
nience store, his mechanic's jacket pulled up over his head.

"Well," said Ms. Hempel. "I think he's dead already."

A howl filled the classroom.

"Usually writers don't publish this type of book until the
main characters have all passed away. So people's feelings
don't get hurt."

Dwight, cold in the ground before the book even reached
the stores. It was the greatest unfairness of all.

"And Rosemary? She's dead? She didn't get to see how
good a writer her son is? She didn't get to see how well he
turned out?" This, too, struck them as terribly unjust.

"No, no," Ms. Hempel said. "Rosemary is still alive. I think. Look in the front pages of your book—he thanks her, he says that she corrected him on certain facts, on the chronology of the events."

"Good." The class looked relieved. "Okay."

An opportunity for moral inquiry presented itself. "If you were writing a book about your life," Ms. Hempel asked, "and you cast a person in an unflattering light, would you wait until that person died? Before you published your book?"

The kids didn't see her point. "I couldn't write a book. I don't have enough to write about, " Simon Grosse said.

"That's not true!" said Ms. Hempel. "Each of you could write a book. Several books, in fact." She tried to remember what Flannery O'Connor had said on the subject. "Anyone who's made it through childhood has enough material to last them until the day they die."

"We haven't made it through yet," Henry Woo said.

"But you will," said Ms. Hempel. "And when you do, you'll have lots to write about. Everyone does interesting things when they're kids."

"And bad things, like Toby?"

"And bad things. Everyone has, even if everyone won't admit it."

The kids waited for a moment, as if they needed, for politeness' sake, to make a show of digesting this information.

"Did you do bad things, Ms. Hempel?"

She should have expected it.

"Well. Be logical. Everyone includes me, doesn't it?"

Greedily the kids leaned forward. "What kinds of bad things?" The back legs of desk-chairs rose into the air.

Ms. Hempel heaved an enormous sigh of resignation. She let her arms drop heavily to her sides. "You really want to know?" she groaned, as if she were finally, under great duress, capitulating to their demands. "You're really going to make me do this?" In truth, she loved talking about herself. Especially to her students.

All heads nodded vigorously.

"I watched TV when I wasn't supposed to. And sometimes I stayed out past my curfew."

The back legs returned to the floor. "That's it?"

"I wasn't always considerate of my parents."

David D'Sousa offered her a wan smile.

"And I pierced my nose with a sewing needle," Ms. Hempel said. "My mother turned her face away every time I walked into the room, like she does when she's watching a violent movie. She was furious at me."

"Caroline Pratt pierced her belly button," Adelaide observed. Caroline was an eighth grader. "She didn't even use ice."

Ms. Hempel shuffled through her collected misdeeds, trying to find ones that she could, in good conscience, share with seventh graders. "I used to like skateboarders. I would help them dye their hair—it made my hands all blotchy. And I was always getting in trouble for breaking the dress code at my school. Once I wore—"

"Ms. Hempel, did you always want to be a teacher?"

It startled her, the conversation veering off in this direction. But then it made sense to her: they believed they already knew the answer. Of course she had always wanted to be a teacher. They were giving her a way out. A way of explaining her unremarkable youth.

"No!" she said. "I certainly didn't."

"Why not?" And the question sounded reproachful. "You like teaching, don't you?" Because suddenly there was the possibility that she didn't. "You like being a teacher. And you were good at school."

They said it with confidence. They treated it as a commonplace, an assumption that needn't be challenged. But the fact that they had said it, the fact that the issue had arisen, in the midst of this tour through Ms. Hempel's offenses, suggested that somewhere, in some part of themselves, they knew differently. It was astonishing, the efficiency with which they arrived at the truth. This was probably why children were so useful in stories and films about social injustice, like *To Kill a Mockingbird*. But Ms. Hempel didn't think that this ability was particularly ennobling. It was just something they could do, the way dogs can hear certain high-pitched sounds, or the way X-rays can see past skin and tissue down to the ghostly blueprint of the bones.

Ms. Hempel sighed. A real one, this time.

"My school—it was demanding, academically. They had very high expectations of us."

"So you were a really good student?"

"No," Ms. Hempel said. "I wasn't."

And this, finally, impressed them.

"I did well on all the standardized tests—like the ERBs?—I scored very high on those. Anything with bubbles I was excellent at, or multiple choice. Even short answer. But it was hard for me to develop my ideas at length. You know, stick with an argument, weave different threads together.

"And my school placed a lot of emphasis on that. On essays, term papers, the final question on exams. It's not because I didn't have anything to say or because I didn't have any ideas. I had lots of them, too many of them. My papers were hard to make sense of.

"Has anyone ever told you that you have lots of potential?

But that you aren't fulfilling it? That's what I heard all throughout high school.

"So I would get terribly nervous before a paper was due. I would tell myself, I'm really going to fulfill my potential on this one. I'm going to make an outline, do a rough draft, write a paragraph a night. I'm going to plan my time effectively. And I would spend two weeks telling myself this, and there I'd be, three o'clock in the morning, the paper's due in five hours, and I can't get my ideas to sit still long enough for me to write any of them down.

"That's why," Ms. Hempel concluded, "I make you turn in your outlines. And your rough drafts. Even though you hate me for it."

But the attempt at levity went unremarked. Her class gazed at her soberly.

"So how'd you become a good student?" Cilla Matsui asked. "How did you get into a good college, and become a teacher?"

"I don't know," Ms. Hempel said. "Worked harder, I guess. What do they say?—I buckled down."

It wasn't until high school that all of this unfulfilled potential was discovered; up until then she had been simply great: great kid, great student. *A pleasure to have in class.* But beginning in the ninth grade, she felt her greatness gently ebbing away, retreating to a cool, deep cistern hidden somewhere inside her. I think it's there! her teachers hollered down into the darkness. It *is* there! her father insisted. But where? she felt like asking. Because there was something faintly suspicious, faintly cajoling, about the way they spoke to her, as if she alone knew the location, and was refusing to tell them for the sake of being contrary.

Dear Parents,

You recently have received an anecdotal about your child. Although it might not have been immediately apparent, this anecdotal was written BY your child, from the perspective of one of his or her teachers. In response to the students' entreaties, I did not include a note of explanation. They wanted to explain the exercise to you themselves, and I hope you have had a chance to talk with your children about the letters they wrote. At this point, though, I would like to offer my own thoughts about the assignment and provide a context in which to understand these "anecdotals."

The assignment was inspired by a passage from the memoir we currently are reading, This Boy's Life *by Tobias Wolff. When this passage occurs, Toby is longing to escape his abusive stepfather and the dead-end town he lives in. When his older brother suggests that Toby apply to boarding school, he becomes excited about the idea, but then discouraged when he realizes that with his poor grades, he will never be accepted. Help arrives in the form of his best friend, who volunteers in the school office and supplies Toby with all the official stationery he needs to create his own letters of recommendation.*

"I felt full of things that had to be said, full of stifled truth. That was what I thought I was writing—the truth. It was truth known only to me, but I believed in it more than I believed in the facts arrayed against it. I believed that in some sense not factually verifiable I was a straight-A student. In the same way, I believed that I was an Eagle Scout, and a powerful swimmer, and a boy of integrity. These were ideas about myself that I had held on to for dear life. Now I gave them voice. . . .

"I wrote without heat or hyperbole, in the words my teachers would have used if they had known me as I knew myself. These were their letters. And in the boy who lived in their letters, the splendid phantom who carried all my hopes, it seemed to me I saw, at last, my own face."

I had hoped that through this exercise students could give voice to their own visions of themselves, visions that might differ from those held by teachers, parents, or friends. I wanted to give them a chance to identify and celebrate what they see as their greatest strengths. During this crucial stage of their development, kids need, I think, to articulate what they believe themselves capable of.

The students approached the assignment with an enthusiasm that overwhelmed me. In their efforts to sound like their teachers, they wrote at greater length, in sharper detail, with more sophisticated phrasing and vocabulary, than they ever have before. Spelling and grammatical errors instantly disappeared; drafts were exhaustively revised. They felt it important that their anecdotals appear convincing.

The decision to mail these anecdotals home was fueled by my desire to share with you these very personal and often revealing self-portraits. When I read them, I found them by turns funny, poignant, and, as Tobias Wolff writes, full of truth. I thought that you, as parents, would value this opportunity to see your children as they see themselves. The intention was not, as I think a few students have mistaken, to play a joke.

I hope that this assignment has offered some meaningful insights into your child, and I deeply regret if it has been the cause of any misunderstanding or distress. Please feel free to contact me if you have further questions or concerns.

Ms. Hempel distributed the letters, each of which she had signed by hand. "Please," she said. "It's imperative that you deliver these to your parents. First thing tonight, before you do anything else. Its contents are extremely important." Though she had omitted certain details: the glee with which she had brandished the school stationery, pulling it out from beneath her cardigan; the instructions she had provided as to perfecting her signature, the way she had leaned over her students' shoulders and adjusted the loops in their Ls. How they had jigged up and down, and laughed wickedly, and rubbed their palms together in a villainous way. How she hadn't the heart to tell them that their anecdotals, so carefully fashioned, would be, upon first glance, apprehended as false.

They didn't sound quite right. And the signatures were awful.

Ms. Hempel had contemplated forgery, once, when she was still a student. Her school instituted a new policy: throughout the semester parents had to sign all tests and papers, so that when final grades were sent home, there wouldn't be any unwelcome surprises. In accordance with the policy, she left her essay on her father's desk, with a little note requesting his signature. The essay had earned a C+.

Later that evening she was lying face down on her bed, air-drying. Her skin was still ruddy from the bath, and as she peeked over her shoulder, surveying the damp expanse of her own body, it reminded her, in a satisfying way, of a walrus. But the comparison wasn't very complimentary. She amended it to a seal, a sleek and shining seal. She imagined a great, gruff hunter coveting her pelt.

But then she was interrupted: the sound of something sliding beneath her door. Disappointingly, only her essay. She padded over from the bed and bent down to retrieve it.

It was horrible to behold. Her father had written not only at the top of the essay, per her instructions, but in the margins as well. His firm handwriting had completely colonized the page. The phrases were mysterious—*No, no, she's being ironic*—agitated and without context, like the cries of people talking in their sleep. Upon closer inspection, she realized that his comments were in response to what her teacher, Mr. Mellis, had already written. To his accusations of *Obscure*, her father rejoined: *Nicely nuanced.* When he wondered how one paragraph connected to the next, her father explained: *It seems a natural transition to move from a general definition to a particular instance.* The dialogue continued until the final page, where her father arrived at his jubilant conclusion: that this was an essay unequaled in its originality, its unpredictable leaps of imagination, its surprising twists and turns. On the bottom of the page, he had printed, neatly: *A–*. It was protected inside a circle.

"Your name!" she bellowed down the staircase. "Why is it so hard for you to just sign your name?"

Back inside her bedroom, she heard the methodical stamp of her father's feet, climbing the stairs. "I don't want any part in this!" she yelled, tucking the essay inside her binder, though she would apologize to Mr. Mellis; she would say, My father lost it.

She stood up and spoke through the crack in the door: "Don't ever do that again."

"I'm sorry, sweetheart," her father said, his voice muffled. He was right on the other side. "But I can't promise you I won't."

It was at that moment forgery first presented itself as an option. But instead she decided to ask, from then on, for her mother's signature. It seemed much easier than fraud. And she knew, anyhow, that even if she did try, she would inevitably get caught. Teachers were alert to that sort of crime.

Ms. Hempel thought that parents would be, too. They were supposed to be vigilant. They were supposed to reprogram the cable box, listen to lyrics, sniff sweaters, check under the mattress. Or, at the least, distinguish between Ms. Hempel's prose and that of a seventh grader. She had read every one of the anecdotals herself, yet she could not account for the lapse.

Some were panegyrics, plain and simple: *Adelaide is without a doubt the most outstanding French student I have ever encountered in my 26 years of teaching.* Some were recantations: *Please ignore my phone call of last week. Matthew is no longer disrupting my class.* Some suggested publication: *Elliott's five-paragraph essay was so superb, I think he should send it to Newsweek.* Some recommended immediate acceleration: *Judging by her excellence in all areas, I think that Emily is ready to take the SATs, and maybe start college early.*

Some anecdotals did everything at once.

Dear Melanie Bean,

I am writing to you about your son. He has been doing exceedingly well in English class. He has gotten a perfect score on every test or quiz we have had in English. He is completely outscoring, outtalking, outparticipating everyone in the class. I look forward to spending my time elaborating his mind in his field of expertise. I would like to consider moving him up to the eighth grade level, which I think would be more suited to his ability. Even though he would miss Spanish every day, I think that Spanish is an inferior class for any person of his mental state, and is simply ruining his skills. I have framed many of his works and

*find them all inspirational, especially his poetry. William
is an inspirational character and I will never forget him. I
suggest that you encourage him to use his skills constantly.*
   Sincerely,
   Beatrice Hempel

Will Bean looked nothing like his mother. He was small
and impish and pale, and had assumed the role of a friendly,
benign irritant, someone who pops up from behind desks and
briskly waves. His greatest joy was a series of books about a
religious community made up of mice, voles, and hedgehogs.
They had taken the Benedictine vows, and created a devout
but merry life for themselves. Will frequently alluded to them.
He produced a radio play in which he performed all the parts:
the sonorous voice of the badger abbot, the tittering of the
field mice, who were still novices and had to work in the mon-
astery's kitchens. He pestered Ms. Hempel into borrowing a
tape deck and making the whole class listen to his production.
In anecdotal terms, he could be described as *whimsical*, or *in-
ventive*, or *delightfully imaginative*.

   Ms. Bean, however, was tall and gaunt and harried. When
Ms. Hempel saw her standing outside the school's gates, she
was swaddled in bags: one for her computer, another for her
dry cleaning, for her groceries, for Will's soccer uniform. It
was strange, how clearly Ms. Hempel could picture her students' lives—Will had tae kwon do on Tuesday afternoons,
and every Wednesday night he spent with his dad—and how
murky their parents' lives seemed by comparison. All she could
see in Ms. Bean was evidence of a job, an exhausting one.

   "Do you have a moment," she said.

   Ms. Hempel said, of course.

"I wanted to speak with you about the assignment."

Would she find it deceitful, and dishonest, as Mrs. Woo did? Or maybe, like Mrs. Galvani, she had telephoned all the relatives, even the ones in California, to tell them the wonderful news. It was unlikely, though, that she loved the assignment, thought it original and brilliant and bold. Only Mr. Radinsky seemed to feel that way.

What Ms. Bean wanted her to know was that she felt the assignment to be unkind. Or maybe not unkind. Maybe just unfair. Because she had been waiting a long time for someone else to finally notice what she had always known about Will. And then to discover that it was an assignment, merely.

The disappointment was terrible—could she understand that?

MR. DUNNE, HER COLLEGE COUNSELOR, was the one who first noticed the discrepancy. Impressive scores, mediocre grades. A specialist was consulted, a series of tests administered, and a medication prescribed. The bitter pills, her father used to call them. The prescription made her hands shake a little, but that wore off after a while. And then: a shy, newfound composure. Her mother entrusted her with the holiday newsletter. She wrote film reviews for the university paper. She had a nice way with words, a neat way of telling a story.

To her ears, though, her stories sounded smushed, as if they had been sat upon by accident. None of the interesting parts survived. Yes, her father flashed the headlights, and yes, she waved at him before she stepped inside. Those details were resilient. Not these: how she waved glamorously, and smiled radiantly, how the headlights heralded the arrival of a star. How her shadow, projected onto the snow, looked huge.

"That was beautiful," her aunt said to her when she returned to her pew. "I can see Oscar doing just that—making sure you got in safely."

Beautiful was not what she intended. Her story was not about safety and concern and anxious attentions. It was a tale of danger, intrigue; a story from the days before her medicine, the days of their collusion, when they communicated in code—click, click—as true accomplices do. When they were still plotting to prove everyone woefully mistaken. This was the story she wanted to tell. Then how did something altogether different emerge? Something she didn't even recognize as her own. Even her father—her coconspirator, her fan—had been changed into someone she didn't quite know. A kind and shadowy figure, sitting in the car. *Benevolent. Thoughtful. Considerate of others.*

Sandman

It was the Annual All-School Safety Assembly. The police officer looked short and lonely in the middle of the stage as he rattled off the possible threats: flashers in raincoats; razor blades in apples; strangers in cars.

Ms. Hempel wanted to raise her hand. Wasn't he forgetting something? He hadn't even mentioned the predators she dreaded most. And wasn't it all supposed to sound more cautionary, more scary?

The grisly details that the officer omitted, Ms. Hempel's imagination generously supplied. The black and shining van, the malevolent clowns, their wigs in sherbet colors. The dim interior, the stains on the carpet. Doors that shut with a hollow slam.

Ms. Hempel clenched her muscles. Terror flowered darkly inside her.

In the very back row of the auditorium, the eighth grade sat and squirmed. Zander, upon completing a drum solo, crashed an invisible cymbal. Elias drew a picture of a small, slouching boy on the back of Julianne's binder. Jonathan, with the toe of his sneaker, battered the chair of the seventh grader sitting in front of him. Here they were, arrayed before her: restless, oblivious, vulnerable, all of them.

"Come on, guys." Mr. Peele, microphone in hand, glowered at the eighth grade. "This is serious."

An assertion that prompted the entire back row to explode into laughter. The eighth graders were banished to their homerooms. As they exited the auditorium, banging into everything they touched, Mr. Peele, his palm clamped over the microphone, instructed the homeroom teachers to finish off the job. "And don't forget to remind them about Safe Haven," he said, but the homeroom teachers were already walking out the door, rolling their eyes at each other. They had inherited yet another mess, like the teaching of sex education, the chaperoning of Trip Days, the organizing of canned-food drives and danceathons.

Ms. Hempel's class, jostling their way back into the homeroom, looked decidedly pleased with themselves. "We're missing French!" Sasha announced. Victoriously, they slammed their backpacks down onto the desk-chairs. "How many more periods until lunch?" Geoffrey asked.

They had no idea of the danger. "Don't you realize," Ms. Hempel cried, shutting the door behind her, "all the terrible things that could happen to you?"

The class regarded her coolly. The whole assembly, they explained, was not for their benefit. They weren't small or cute enough anymore. They were too wised-up. "Want some candy, little girl?" Elias said in a cooing voice. Who would fall for such a stupid trick? Probably even the fifth and sixth graders knew better.

"I mean," Sasha said, "we're not exactly the ones to worry about."

"I know!" A chorus of agreement. And then, the cherished

complaint: no one seemed to have noticed the fact that they were, virtually, in high school and thus fully capable of handling their own affairs.

"Haven't you heard," persisted Ms. Hempel, "about the clowns? Who kidnap you? Who drive around in vans!"

"Oh, Ms. Hempel," Julianne sighed. "We're fine. Really."

"Can you imagine," Sasha asked, "a clown taking off with Jonathan Hamish?"

The class turned and looked at Jonathan, who had peeled the sole off his sneaker and was now trying to insert it down the back of Theo's shirt. The logic went: in the unlikely chance that Jonathan could be swayed by the promise of bottle rockets and lured into the back of a dark and fusty van, he would exhaust the clowns before anything creepy might happen. The kids chuckled at the thought: the clowns slumped over, wigs askew, wearing the same dazed, disbelieving expression they sometimes saw on the faces of Jonathan's teachers.

Meanwhile, Theo wriggled valorously.

Ms. Hempel confiscated the sole.

"What is Jonathan, or any of you, going to do when the clowns sneak up behind you and clobber you over the head with a tire iron?" she asked. "Or stuff a chloroform-soaked towel underneath your nose, and you pass out? Dead to the world? What are you going to do then?"

"They do that?" Geoffrey asked.

"For real?" Julianne asked.

"Yes!" Ms. Hempel said. "I read it in the newspaper."

The eighth grade looked appalled. Ms. Hempel felt appalled, at the enormity of her lie. Generally speaking, her lying was of the mildest sort, only because she couldn't do it very well. A genetic failing. Her father was a terrible liar. "Did you get in touch with the insurance man?" her mother would

ask, and he would answer, "Yes!" in a confident way that made
it quite clear he had not. Once, when he picked her up from
school, more than forty-five minutes late, he had glared at
the dashboard and growled, "Emergency at the hospital," even
though his damp tennis shorts in the backseat were letting off
a most powerful reek.

But he was scrupulously honest about important things.
When faced with a difficult question, he never lied or dodged
or even faltered. "Toxic shock syndrome," he once explained
to her, "occurs when a woman leaves a tampon or an IUD inside her vagina for too long, allowing bacteria to gather. The
bacteria then causes an infection that enters her bloodstream
and can, but not always, result in her immediate death." Mas-
tectomy and herpes were described just as clearly.

It was a model she admired. "Sodomy," Ms. Hempel now
said to her class, "is what's happening in the back of those
vans. And though sodomy is a word that can be used in ref-
erence to any sort of sexual intercourse, it most commonly
refers to anal sex."

They seemed to have a good understanding of what that
was. Roderick made a joke about taking a shower and having
to pick up a bar of soap off the floor. The class laughed warily.
They shifted in their desk-chairs.

"The clowns do this to you while you're unconscious?"
Theo asked.

"Exactly," Ms. Hempel said, and the kids fell silent. The
other clowns, the ridiculous ones wearing wigs and clutching
candy, had been replaced: these new ones marched through
the homeroom swinging their tire irons, waving their towels,
unbuckling their pants.

"So do you see why we're scared? Why we want you to be
careful?"

The kids nodded. They seemed to have gone suddenly limp. Ms. Hempel felt horrible.

"But don't worry!" she said. "There are stickers everywhere. You've seen them. The blue ones? With the little lighthouse on them."

"Safe Haven," said Sasha dully.

"Right!" Ms. Hempel said. "If you see that sticker in a store window, you know that you can walk inside and they'll take care of you and call the police and call your parents."

"You mean if the clowns try to clobber us," Zander clarified.

"Or if anyone strange approaches you," she said. "Anyone who makes you feel uncomfortable."

"But Safe Haven doesn't work!" Gloria said. "When this gross guy was following me home from the bus stop, I went into Video Connection, and the girl there didn't even know what I was talking about."

"A gross guy followed you home?" Ms. Hempel asked.

"He kept singing, *You are the sun, you are the rain*, really quietly, just so I could hear. You know that song?"

The other girls squealed softly in disgust.

"When did this happen?" Ms. Hempel asked.

"It happens all the time!" the girls cried out, and like a flock of startled pigeons they seemed to all rise up at once. Didn't Ms. Hempel know? Weirdness was lurking everywhere: behind the bank, holding a broom; on the subway, grazing your butt; at the park, asking if he could maybe touch your hair. *What book are you reading? What grade are you in?* The girls bounced up and down in their chairs, seething, commiserating, trying to outdo each other. When I was walking to school. When I was visiting my cousin. No, wait! Listen: When I was, like, twelve. . . .

Homeroom discussions always seemed to end this way. The girls in a glorious fury; the boys gazing dumbly at the carpet. What would possess a clown, Ms. Hempel wondered, to kidnap one of these beautiful girls? So lively, and smart, and suspicious. Such strong legs, from kicking soccer balls and making jump shots. So full of outrage.

The boys, though: brash and bewildered, oddly proportioned. Some of them were finally beginning to grow tall. They wore voluminous pants that hung precariously on their hips. They grinned readily. During the winter, when it was very cold, they refused to wear their coats in the yard: We get hot when we run around! they said. Their T-shirts flapped against their thin arms; their chests heaved. The ball rarely made it into the net, but they didn't seem to mind. It was all about the hurling and the frenzied grasping and the thundering down to the other end of the court. And even though the girls were always plucking at Ms. Hempel's sleeve, demanding that she listen, it was the boys who tugged at her heart, who seemed to her the ripest for abduction.

Ms. Hempel wondered if her story of that morning could be true, or if it were, factually speaking, impossible. The detail about chloroform bothered her; it struck her as transparently dramatic, like a woman who dashes about with a long, fragile scarf fluttering behind her. It was an anachronism; something from the days of white slavery, and opium smuggling, and jewel heists. Where had she learned about chloroform, anyway? Probably Tintin.

"If you wanted to kidnap someone, what would you use?" she asked Amit. They were lying in bed, with the lights off. "To knock them unconscious. So that you could drag them into the back of your van."

"Chloroform, I guess."

"Really?" She brightened. It made her happy that the person she was marrying would commit crimes in the same way as she would. "There isn't anything more modern you would use? Aren't there all sorts of new chemicals?"

"No, I think chloroform would do the trick," he said.

"Good," she said. "That's what I thought, too."

"Are you planning on kidnapping anyone?" he asked.

"Maybe."

Then, "Of course not!" she said, and laughed, and slapped him on the arm. They settled into each other.

She had gone to the same high school as Amit, even graduated the same year, but they had barely spoken then. She remembered him as black-haired and elfin and somewhat aloof: in an innocent, not a superior, way. His one distinguishing trait had been his devotion to cross-country running. Sometimes her car pool passed him on the road, and she would lean her forehead against the cool glass, wondering how many miles he had already covered and feeling glad that she was splayed across the backseat of a station wagon. She never once saw him panting; it seemed as if he could bound along interminably. Both of her best friends had seen his penis. As part of a short-lived weight-loss regimen, they had joined the cross-country team, and as they straddled the lawn, stretching their muscles, they glimpsed the head of his penis, appearing from beneath the edge of his delicate, shimmering shorts.

When she saw him again, years later, this detail reared up before her as soon as she sat down beside him. It was an alumni event, an idea that embarrassed her, but her school had reserved seats at a French-Canadian circus that she badly wanted to see. Amit was there, he said, for exactly the same reason. They discovered many other things in common: warm feelings for Mrs. Kravatz, the biology teacher; a passion for the novels of Thomas Hardy; regret that they hadn't joined a circus themselves. They admitted to each other that even though, as students, they had regarded their high school as detestable and oppressive, they now sometimes caught themselves yearning for it.

The circus, too, filled her with longing. As soon as the lights fell, and the audience hushed, and the circus master appeared barking out his welcome, and the acrobats came tumbling into the ring, and the quaint little orchestra struck up its tinkling song, and the lovely women pranced about with thin velvet ribbons tied around their necks, as soon as all this began, she felt herself missing the circus even as it unfolded before her. Folded and unfolded—this circus was famous for its contortionists. But what they did seemed like the most normal thing in the world; their bodies, glittering in the blue light, appeared enormously relieved, as if they had been permitted, finally, to relax into their most natural states. Clearly she saw how the feet longed to roost behind the ears, how the spine was as stretchy as chewing gum. It made her feel sorry for her own creaking vessel, shuffling along dimly, made to stand upright on two feet. No, not vessel—because if this circus, so full of secrets, revealed anything, it was that the body does not contain, but is contained; rather than comb through the jungles of Asia and Africa and bring back, in shackles, the wildlife found there, this circus had coaxed out of hiding a strange beast, the body.

"Oh, those Canadians!" she murmured, and Amit nodded ardently, as if he understood precisely what she wasn't able to say.

It was the circus, she felt sure, that had made possible all that followed. Where else but in the company of acrobats could she imagine her own body fitting with his? Watching him from the station wagon, his black hair, his small frame skimming along the road, she could not have imagined it. Her imagination would have balked, recoiled: why, she wasn't sure. But it was subdued now, compliant; she sat beside him at the circus and the unimaginable became suddenly, forcefully possible. Everything else seemed easy: the long correspondence, the breaking off with his girlfriend, the bringing together of their two libraries.

And his penis she forgot all about, even after she had herself encountered it. Her two best friends had to remind her of the story.

HER BEST FRIENDS, GRETA AND KATE, had their hearts set on a bridal shower. It was held at a Victorian tearoom, with mismatched china and plates of watercress sandwiches. Only the three of them were invited.

In a wobbly rattan chair, her legs firmly planted, sat Kate. "Don't sit there," she said to Greta. "Floral chintz is for Beatrice. The Angel in the House."

Greta tucked herself into a wing chair. With a great show of ceremony, she unclipped her beeper and stuffed it deep inside her purse. "No interruptions!" she declared. The symmetry was pleasing: a doctor, a lawyer, a teacher, the professions you aspire to when you're a child, before you learn about all the other possibilities.

"Ooooh, look at you!" Greta said to Beatrice, who had removed her sweater.

Beatrice looked down at her breasts. "Do you think it's too much?"

"No!" they said at once.

"You wore that to school?" Greta asked, and Beatrice nodded.

"Those poor boys," said Kate, reaching for the sugar cubes.

"Pup tent!" Greta cried, and though Beatrice tried to protest, tried to explain that her students didn't look at her that way, that they were inflamed by other teachers like Ms. Burnes, who taught science, and Madame Planchon, who wore seamed stockings, her two best friends were already slapping hands above the teapot.

"Your breasts are *lovely*." Greta leaned over and squeezed Beatrice's leg. "You *should* show them off."

"Absolutely," Kate said.

This type of flattery—excessive, heartfelt, slightly barbed—was their favorite activity. They served as each other's most passionate advocates: no one, in Beatrice's mind, was as intelligent and beautiful and kind and brave and talented as Kate and Greta. And Kate and Greta, in turn, would insist the same of Beatrice. It was puzzling, then, that together they had managed to collect such a number of men who seemed less alert to these qualities. Amit was a departure in this regard. And Beatrice wondered if she might be a disappointment to her friends, not because she was getting married, but because she had stopped falling in love with men who were childlike, or ill-tempered, or flat-footed, or unkind. Or maybe simply indifferent.

Which was not at all what they had planned when they were in high school. These plans had imagined graceful men with slim hips and luminous skin. At least that was what Greta described. The fact that he might be gay to begin with would only make his conversion all the more remarkable. Kate wanted a looming, overpowering man, one who could make her feel petite (for once) and envelop her entirely. And then? A nighttime wedding, with Japanese lanterns. Quails and asparagus. A honeymoon in Prague. Nearly every lunch period was spent in this fashion. Pushing their trays to one side, they huddled over the table and spangled their futures with intrigues and travels and children and accolades. For the sake of realism, they threw in obstacles: a callous lover for Kate (she eventually comes to her senses); Beatrice's close call with pharmaceuticals (from which she emerges chastened, but stronger). Then they liked to skip far ahead and picture themselves on a porch, widowed, delighting in each other's company once again.

Now, having arrived at the future, they liked nothing better than to recall their days around the lunch table. They exclaimed over their miscalculations. Holding up their tearoom selves and measuring them against their lunchroom selves, they tried to account for the discrepancies. How did wild-eyed Beatrice become a teacher? How did she succeed in getting engaged before anyone else? The trajectory was not at all what they had predicted.

"Who would have thought," Greta asked, loosening a strawberry from its stem, "that you would marry Amit Hawkins?"

"Can you imagine," Kate said, "sitting there in practice and knowing, That penis, one day, is going to penetrate our beloved Bea."

"I bet he never would have dreamt it," Greta said.

"Did he?" Kate asked, excited. "Did he notice you then?"

Beatrice had asked him that very question, even though she felt it vain and somewhat despicable to do so.

"Oh no, not in that way. He was scared of me."

"He was?" Kate and Greta laughed.

"Yes!" Beatrice said. "I can see why."

Her infected nose piercing. Her scarlet bra straps. Her eagerness to take off her clothes: for the spring play, for the advanced photography class, for any tedious game of Truth or Dare. Her fits of weeping. Her steel-toed boots. Her term papers on "Edie Sedgwick: Little Girl Lost" and "Get Your Motors Running: The Rise and Fall of the Hells Angels." A quote on her yearbook page from the Marquis de Sade.

"But who could be scared of Ms. Hempel?" Kate asked, cheerfully.

"Speaking of which—we have a present for you!" Greta said and dove beneath the tea table.

Kate cleared a space in front in Beatrice: "Whenever you wear it, you must think of us."

Greta resurfaced, beaming, and brandishing a box.

"Open it!"

Carefully Beatrice tugged at the bow, lifted the lid, burrowed through the crackling tissue paper.

"What is it?" she asked.

"Keep going," Kate said. "It's in there somewhere."

She felt something slippery and grabbed it.

"What can it be?" she asked, as she imagined, very clearly, a silk nightgown. She pulled her present from its box.

Greta and Kate shrieked. "Do you love them?"

Beatrice nodded.

"Crotchless panties!" they cried, and clapped their hands, as if applauding all the stunts she would perform while wearing them.

They weren't at all silky. Beatrice brushed her cheek against them: 100 percent polyester. And smelling of something sweetly, sickly rubbery.

The saucers rattled. Greta leaned forward, dunking her lovely beads into her cup. "Do you like them? Really?"

Beatrice smiled bravely. "They're perfect," she said, though they absolutely weren't. They were woefully inadequate. Not up to the task.

"I hope they won't shock Amit," Greta said, as Beatrice gently returned them to their box. She looked up from the present at her two best friends, her two talented, brilliant, unintuitive friends. They had no idea.

If someone had asked, Beatrice might have described her notion of sex thus: warm bodies in the dark, sighing and rustling, then arcing up in perfect tandem, like synchronized swimmers. Amit's concept involved something much more strenuous and well lit and out of the ordinary. His requests often alarmed her. She knew the crotchless panties would strike him as silly, or simply beside the point. This thought made her feel sad, both sad and spooked.

Even worse, she felt duplicitous, as though she had worked on him an unforgivable deception. He now carried about with him a baffled, slightly disappointed air. But she couldn't help it: how her body clenched, how the alarm was raised, how her every muscle responded with a panicked shout of *Sodomy!* He had mistaken her for something else entirely, and who could blame him? The scarlet bra straps, the Marquis de Sade. The fondness for acrobats.

She wondered at what point his appetite had turned. As far as she understood, an interest in anal sex was not something one was born with. She imagined an early, unsuccessful coupling; flickering filmstrips; a summer spent in Europe. All it took were some crooked signposts, some conspiracy of events and influences. Because he couldn't have always wanted this. Why hadn't she stopped the car? Why hadn't she sprung out of the station wagon and loved him then? When a kiss was a surprise, the introduction of tongue an astonishment. When a small, black-haired boy would have swooned at the thought of her underwear. Would have died, nearly, at the touch of her hands, her chewing gum breath, her permission to enter. It would have been enough; it would have been the whole world, then.

So much more was asked of her now. Stamina, flexibility, imagination (or, perhaps, a quieting of her imagination). A willingness to endure, and to enjoy, what she feared would be a rupturing pain. It all made her feel exhausted and very far away from him, as if he were standing atop a flight of stairs and she were stranded at the bottom, too breathless to climb up. Even though he waited there, full of love, full of patience, full of expectancy, she wondered how long it would be before he stretched out his hamstrings, took a deep breath, and bounded off.

But maybe she was remembering it all wrong; maybe there was never a time when a kiss could stun and astonish. Maybe, if she aligned the years correctly, she would discover that while Amit was devoting himself to cross-country running, Greta was contorted (the true contortionist) over the stick shift in her mother's car, offering an illustration of how to manage a penis inside one's mouth, and Beatrice was sitting in the backseat, watching very closely. Greta, who now leaned across the tea table and grasped Beatrice's hand and said, suddenly, "We love you so much, Bea."

To Beatrice's surprise, Amit liked the crotchless panties. He wore them on his head and danced around the apartment. *All of me*, he sang. *Why not take all of me.*

He sang and danced with his eyes closed. He snatched her up, and held her close, and, with a snap of his wrist, unfurled her. She dangled out in space, teetering on her tiptoes, ready to crash into the snake tank—but then he spooled her back in again. Together they danced wildly. They dipped and spun and almost knocked over a lamp. He tried to lift her off the floor, but he wasn't quite tall enough, so she gave a little push and folded up her legs, and it was nearly the same as being swept off her feet.

Can't you see, he sang. *I'm no good without you.*

She hung on to his neck and they waltzed over her pop quizzes. And into the bookcase, where he stumbled, and books toppled, and he pulled away from her, doubled over. She stooped down to help and suddenly he shot up, taking her with him, slung over his shoulder like a squalling child. She flailed and shrieked. Staggering about the room, Amit huffed, *You took the part that once was my heart.*

With a thump, he deposited her onto the sofa. *So why not take all of me?*

He then twirled around and lurched down the hallway and out the door. To buy them two bottles of ginger ale.

Beatrice lolled on the sofa and hummed a coda to his song. What luck! What fortune! A thousand blessings had been bestowed upon her. A springy sofa, a clean apartment. A pile of pop quizzes that could wait until morning. A dancing fiancé. An airborne Beatrice. A pair of best friends, and a beautiful bridal shower.

Abruptly, she stiffened. For where was her present? Still perched atop her fiancé's head. Preening itself. And ruffling its polyester feathers.

And where was her fiancé? Walking down the avenue, with a small lilt, a small stutter, in his step.

Beatrice retrieved her shoes from beneath the sofa and ran out into the street. She looked both ways. She saw a Dumpster, a dark alley, and a brand-new van with a voluptuous woman painted on its side. She didn't see Amit. She didn't see anyone on the street, as if she had rushed out of their apartment and into her own bad dream.

Her nightmares took a truly frightening turn when she was ten, and her father began to appear in them, to save her. But she always knew, through the inevitable logic of nightmares, that her father would be destroyed, that he would struggle valiantly but to no avail, and that his knees would crumble and his eyes would dim and he might try to speak a few loving, gurgling words to her before he expired. She knew it with an awful, churning certainty. It didn't matter what shape the menace took: sometimes it was a sticky pink substance that came bubbling under the door; sometimes it was an infernal drug lord, disguised as her principal, who was trying to bring her school under his narcotic control. These terrors were acute, yet relatively benign, as long as she was battling them by herself. Once her father got involved, the nightmares would escalate: for what was more paralyzing than the sight of your father, corroding in acid, pinned down by a pitchfork, drooling and drug addled? In one dream she sat in the back of his car and watched his eyes in the rearview mirror as he slowly melted into his seat.

Beatrice hurried down the street. She passed a ladder, a trash can, a pool of broken glass.

In her dreams, death always took her father by surprise. Even up until the very end, he'd remain convinced of his immunity. With this same conviction he would, in real life, pick fights with fellow motorists, climb up onto the roof rather than call the handyman, and disappear into the wilderness for whole days at a time. Beatrice found these weekend excursions particularly infuriating. What better way to court calamity than canoeing? She had seen movies; she knew about the dangers. The willful rapids, the bears snuffling about the campsite, the invisible parasites infesting the water. Not to mention the belligerent, banjo-picking locals who would immediately recognize her father for the city-slicking, fancy-pants doctor he was. She would try to tempt him with alluring alternatives: "We could go to the mall," she'd say, "get some of those soft pretzels that you like." Or she would volunteer to help him load up the car, and then tell him mournful stories about a girl in her class, whose grades—due to her father's death in a tragic canoeing accident—had experienced a precipitous decline. But these tactics rarely worked.

Her mother didn't want him to leave, either. She would not make him sandwiches to eat on the road; she would not smile; sometimes she wouldn't even appear in the driveway to say good-bye. On the weekends that Beatrice's father went away, she and her mother would catch glimpses of one another as they each stalked about the house in an undisturbed rage. But when the telephone rang, her mother, answering it, would say gaily, "Oscar? He's off canoeing!" And somehow, the way she said it—in a bright, emphatic tone that left no room for further questions—made it seem as if Beatrice's father were right there with them, uttering the words himself. She spoke in the voice he always used when asserting what was most obviously untrue. The effect was strange—hearing this voice come out of her mother. Then, with a slight shrug, she would return to herself, her face slackening, her pen circling the telephone pad, and Beatrice, confronted with the mystery of her father, the mystery of her mother, could only write repeatedly, in ever tinier cursive, *Canoeing is a perilous outdoor sport.* She wrote it five times on the last page of her science notebook, stopped, remembered herself, and neatly tore out the page; at the end of every two weeks you had to turn in your notebook for a grade.

By Monday morning he would be back again, in time to make Beatrice breakfast and deliver her to school. She softened at the sight of him standing there in the kitchen, flushed and rumpled and stubbled, placing her favorite antique spoon on the table. The wilderness had released him, had given him back. And, just like that, all her fury would be snuffed out. Any irritation was now redirected at her mother, who upon his return had camped out in her bathtub, listening to NPR at a deafening volume. She should come downstairs! Beatrice would silently fume. She should come fluttering in, full of kisses and gratitude and relief!

Disaster had been held off once again. Wasn't that cause for rejoicing?

For there Amit was, waiting in the checkout line, his small black head shining above the magazine racks. No crotchless panties in sight. Beatrice stood on the sidewalk and watched him pay for the two bottles of ginger ale. What luck, she felt. What extraordinary fortune.

THE EIGHTH GRADERS WERE less fortunate. The next morning dawned drearily, with assurances from the weatherwoman that the sky would remain overcast. The sky was always overcast on Trip Day, the one day out of the whole year when the eighth grade took a very long bus ride to a rather grimy beach. They showed no signs of discouragement, however. Even at the stoplights, the school bus rocked back and forth crazily.

"Rule Number One!" Ms. Hempel hollered, before she let them disembark. "Don't go in past your waist. There's only one lifeguard on duty. And don't forget to wear sunscreen. Those ultraviolet rays will burn you up, even though it's cloudy!"

"And don't talk to clowns," someone shouted from the back.

"Right," Ms. Hempel said.

The eighth grade clattered off the bus and, without awaiting further orders, stormed the beach. Ms. Hempel and the three other homeroom teachers trudged grimly behind, trying to balance between them the poles for a volleyball net. Yelps could already be heard from the water.

As they cleared the boardwalk, Ms. Hempel saw her students frisking bravely in the surf. It was still very cold out. Some girls wore cheeky little two-pieces flecked with polka dots and daisies; others skulked about in their fathers' T-shirts. The boys were already immersed up to their necks, their sleek heads bobbing atop the waves. "It's freezing!" the girls wailed. "Ms. Hempel! It's freezing!"

Ms. Hempel held their towels in her outstretched arms and rubbed their backs when they scrambled, dripping, up from the water. The girls clustered about her, reaching out their trembling hands and pressing them against her cheek: "See?" they asked. "See how cold I am!"

"Brrrrrr!" Ms. Hempel said, and rubbed them harder.

The girls then arranged their towels into a beautiful mosaic on the sand. Dropping down upon their knees, they dug into their beach bags, emerging with plastic containers and painted tins and shoe boxes lined with waxed paper. These they gravely placed in the middle of the mosaic. Julianne circled about them, distributing paper plates, while Keisha handed out Dixie cups half filled with soda. One by one the lids were removed, revealing jerked chicken, fruit salad, crumbling banana bread, couscous, fried plantains, sesame noodles, sticky little rice balls. The girls fell upon the food. "We organized a potluck," Sasha explained, forking a pineapple wedge and making room for Ms. Hempel. "Please help yourself."

Meanwhile, the boys had straggled up onto the beach and were now huddled around the school cooler, peering down into sodden paper bags. They consoled themselves by clapping their sacks of school-issued potato chips and making them explode.

"They thought a potluck was stupid," Alice said, with profound satisfaction.

A family of seagulls and the three other homeroom teachers patrolled the area. Ms. Hempel shouted out, "Everything's okay over here!" and accepted a lemon square, reminding herself that her presence was required. She would make sure that no paper plates were left in the sand. She would apply sunscreen to the girls' shoulders, and provide an adult perspective on their discussions. Drowsily, she gazed out at the ocean. "I can't believe you went in," she murmured.

The morning passed slowly. Swimming and lunch had already taken place, and it wasn't even eleven yet. No one dared return to the water; common sense had set in. And the volleyball net kept collapsing. The girls wrapped themselves in their towels and asked Ms. Hempel personal questions. Was she wearing, underneath her sweater, a one-piece or a two-piece? Did she propose or did he? But everything she said seemed only to remind them of something more urgent that they needed to say. Each one of her answers was interrupted, and then abandoned, as the girls hurried from one new topic to the next: discriminatory gym teachers; open-minded parents; plus-sized models. The animated nature of the discussion kept them warm. When they wanted to make a point, they threw off their towels, baring themselves like superheroes.

Ms. Hempel found herself noticing a group of boys off in the distance, bending themselves to a task with a suspicious degree of concentration. "What do you think they're doing?" she asked.

"Who knows?" Gloria sighed.

"Maybe I should go check on them," Ms. Hempel said.

"They're fine," Julianne said, a bit sternly.

But they didn't look fine. They were crouching over something. Maybe they had found a stash of hypodermic needles, washed up by the tide.

"I had better go see," Ms. Hempel said.

"Ms. Hempel . . . ," the girls called, but she was already on her feet and walking away from them.

Upon closer inspection, she saw that the boys were absorbed in a fairly harmless activity. It involved one boy lying down on his back, the other boys heaping sand on top of him and patting it down, and then the boy heaving himself up and lumbering to his feet. The boys took great care to smooth out the sand so that when the body began to stir, the grave would crack and fissure in a dramatic fashion. She wasn't sure where the pleasure lay: in burying a classmate, or in freeing oneself from the sand. They attacked both roles with equal gusto. She stood to one side and watched them.

When it was Jonathan Hamish's turn, the boys began to add, at his behest, anatomy to his burial mound. As they shaped two sandy breasts, they glanced over at Ms. Hempel, to see what she would do. Their glance both defied and invited reproach, a look with which she was very familiar. She smiled at them permissively, then rolled her eyes to show how unflappable she was. An argument arose as to the size of the outcroppings: some boys, among them Elias and Theo, felt they should be round and realistic, while others, like Roderick, wanted to keep building the breasts until they sat high and pointy on Jonathan's chest. "That's not what they do," Elias muttered, but sand was an imprecise medium to begin with. Jonathan grinned down at his protrusions.

The breasts turned out so well the boys decided to add a penis. They glanced over, again, in Ms. Hempel's direction. They even cleared a little space for her so she could stump over to the penis and object. But didn't they know? She was the young teacher. It was her job to indulge them, to be impervious to shock, to watch all the same television shows that they did. She laughed when they made off-color jokes. She allowed them to use curse words in their creative writing. She taught sex education with unheard-of candor. Of course, they were constantly testing her. When she asked her homeroom to anonymously submit any question, any question at all, regarding puberty or sex or contraception, she received some very graphic queries. She stood at the front of the class and read each question aloud. Competently, intrepidly, she described the consistency of semen, what purpose lubricant served, why a woman might enjoy receiving oral sex.

Jonathan Hamish, who didn't even try to disguise his handwriting, had submitted a question of a more challenging sort. He grinned at her when he saw that she had pulled his crumpled paper from the pile. *Whose the best lover you've ever had?* Jonathan watched her closely, as if waiting for her to discard it, frown at him, send him downstairs to Mr. Peele's office. But she found herself mysteriously touched, felt herself blushing in a pleasurable way. Another word, surely, would have been the more obvious choice: What's the best sex you've ever had? Who's the best fuck? But even in his efforts to provoke her, he had selected a word that was exceedingly charming. Full of solicitous, gentlemanly concern. And he grinned at her—not devilishly, not leeringly—but sweetly almost, sweetly and frankly. As if he really wanted to know. As if he were asking only because all aspects of her life were of interest to him. As if the thought of her embroiled in sweaty sex were unimaginable. In Jonathan Hamish's view of the world, Ms. Hempel would make love.

When she read the question aloud, the homeroom swiveled in their seats and glared at Jonathan. They knew that only he would ask such a question.

"Well," Ms. Hempel said, displaying her ring finger. "Shouldn't the answer be obvious?"

THE PENIS, HAVING A MORE slender base, proved more difficult than the breasts. It kept on toppling over. After a few frustrated attempts, the boys settled on a suggestive hillock (a pup tent, Ms. Hempel realized). They stepped back and admired their handiwork.

"Keep going," Jonathan commanded, waggling his hands and feet. "I'm not completely covered."

They heaped more sand upon him, making it necessary that he remain absolutely still, for even the smallest twitch of his fingers could disrupt their progress. Jonathan, as Ms. Hempel well knew, was a child unable to stop moving. And perhaps it was a relief to him, this stillness, this weight pressing down on him.

But he still was not satisfied with the effect. "Try putting more sand on my neck, and up around my ears," he instructed.

The other boys squatted down beside his head and carefully shaped the sand. "More," Jonathan said. "It doesn't feel right."

He could no longer move his head, but his eyes darted back and forth, monitoring their efforts. "You can put more on my forehead, and my chin," he said. "Get as much on my face as you can."

His voice kept getting quieter and quieter. Ms. Hempel peered down at him anxiously. "Are you all right in there?" she asked. "Jonathan, do you want them to stop?"

Finally, in a very small voice, he said, "Enough."

The boys were proud of what they had done. "Picture!" Roderick yelled. "We have to take a picture!" None of the boys had brought a camera. Only the girls had thought to do that. So off they went, thundering down the beach. "Don't move!" they shouted back at Jonathan.

"Okay," he whispered.

Ms. Hempel knelt down beside him. "Jonathan," she said. "Are you really okay?"

"I'm okay," he whispered. His mouth had turned a funny dark color, as if he had just finished eating a grape Popsicle.

"Promise me."

"I'm just resting," he said, and closed his eyes.

"Jonathan?" she asked. "Do you want me to get you anything? Do you want some water?"

"No," he sighed, his eyes still closed.

Then he asked, "Do you see them?"

"They'll be back any minute now," she said. "It's not very far."

"This sand is heavy," he whispered.

"Do you want to get up?" she asked. "Jonathan?"

"I'm okay. It's just a little hard to breathe."

"Oh, sweetheart," she said. "That doesn't sound good."

"It's okay," he whispered. "Are they back yet?"

But only Ms. DeWitt appeared on the horizon: teacher of advanced math, coach of girls' basketball. When she called out, Ms. Hempel waved back at her and smiled.

"Everything's fine!" she shouted, despairingly.

Another teacher would have intervened, she knew, would have brought it all to a halt. *Stand up*, she imagined Ms. De-Witt barking. *Right now. This is dangerous.*

Words that Ms. Hempel should have said from the very beginning.

"Can you see them?" Jonathan whispered.

"Yes," she told him, though it wasn't true. "They're running straight at us."

THE BOYS RETURNED, EVENTUALLY, and the picture was taken. Jonathan had become quite blue by that point. He wasn't able to burst forth from the sand as the others had. It was much more of a struggle for him, and when he pulled himself to his feet, he was shivering violently. The other boys draped him in their towels. "Let's go back to the bus," Ms. Hempel said. "We can ask the bus driver to turn on the heater."

Together they climbed up the beach toward the parking lot. The boys ran ahead and tripped each other and kicked sand, but Jonathan walked behind them, still trembling, a towel thrown over his head like a hood. Ms. Hempel made him stop.

"Come here," she said, and she held him.

Creep

As children, Beatrice and her brother lived on the very top floor of their house, in rooms that had been inhabited by servants nearly one hundred years before. Attached to the wall at the top of the stairs was a beautiful wooden box, with one side made of glass, and painted upon the glass, in tiny gold letters, were the names of rooms: MASTER BEDROOM; BUTLER'S PANTRY; DINING ROOM; CONSERVATORY; LOGGIA. Through the glass you could see a complicated system of hammers and bells and cogs, strung together with bright copper wiring that disappeared through a hole in the bottom corner of the box and burrowed into the house's thick walls, only to emerge on the floors below, inside each of the gold-lettered rooms, in the form of a button. The finger most often pressing the button was Beatrice's, for when you pressed it, an electric current would course up the copper wiring to the top floor of the house, and a little bell inside the wooden box would ring, not a tinkling ring, but a sort of low-pitched vibration, similar to the sound people make when they're cold: Brrrrrrrrrrr.

Beatrice never got tired of hearing this sound. She liked it so much, she invented a game called Servant: she would waft into a room, drape herself across a chair, and then, in a gesture both impatient and languid, poke the little button embedded in the wall. She would hear, very faintly, that low and lovely hum, and then the muffled drumbeat of her brother hurrying down the four flights of stairs. "How may I be of service, madam?" he had to ask, according to the rules. She would tell him, "I'm dying for a glass of water. On a tray," or "Would you mind terribly, opening the curtains?" and depending upon how well he performed the tasks, a new round would begin, with Calvin climbing back up the stairs to wait beside the box and Beatrice deciding which room she would waft into next. But this was only one of many games she had invented, and maybe not as good as Teacher, or Dead, or Blackout.

Living, as they did, at the top of the house, Beatrice and her brother were surrounded by trees. In the summer, their rooms filled with a green light. In the winter, the fir boughs grew heavy with snow and brushed against their windowpanes. Because they lived in rooms meant only for servants, their windows were small and perfectly square, not long and grand like those in the rest of the house. But they preferred it this way: They liked living in their tiny rooms, aloft in the trees; they liked the green light falling in squares at their feet. Their rooms were almost the same, but not quite: Calvin had a fireplace in his, and Beatrice had a wall of bookshelves built into hers.

Beatrice didn't read books anymore. All she did was listen to the radio. She listened late at night, to the pirate stations found at the bottom of the dial. In the place where books should have been, she kept her tremendous radio. It had once belonged to her mother, in the days when she still wore her hair long and wrote essays.

The pirate radio stations broadcast many different shows: they had names such as the Flophouse, and Nocturnal

Emissions, and the Curious Sofa. Beatrice's favorite was a program called the Rock Hotel. It came on every night at eleven
o'clock and played music of the sort that Beatrice had never
heard before, music that sounded at once grinding and frenzied,
like a train car screeching backward down a mountain, and
all the passengers inside howling. A velvety static blanketed
everything, like snow falling on the scene of the disaster. Before
discovering the Rock Hotel, Beatrice had believed that music
was supposed to make things more beautiful and orderly.

That's when I reach for my revolver, she sang in the bathroom. *That's when it all just slips away.*

Calvin stood outside the door. "What are you doing?" he
asked.

She threw the door open and lunged forward, her hand
convulsing. "I'm practicing electric guitar," she said.

Calvin tucked his chin against his shoulder and cocked
his wrist in the air; he drew an invisible bow across invisible
strings. "I will accompany you."

Beatrice let her hands drop. For a moment she felt poi-
soned. But it was no use explaining that violins and guitars
don't go together. She knew what he would say, serenely: "It's
an *electric* violin."

She wheeled to face the mirror hanging over the sink.
"Give me a sword," she said.

"Viking, Roman, or Greek?" Calvin asked.

"Viking!" Beatrice said. Her brother returned with the
sword. Wielding it over her head, she studied herself in the
mirror. Her arms, raised this way, looked thinner than they
did when just hanging at her sides. She wondered what other
reasons she might find to assume this position. "Tremble!" she
said, to no one in particular.

Calvin wedged himself between her and the sink, so that

he could brush his teeth. He brushed his teeth many times a day because he was concerned about plaque. On his birthday their mother had given him a kit containing a special yellow solution and a special handheld light. You sloshed the solution inside your mouth, made the bathroom completely dark, flicked on the special light, and saw, in beautiful and arctic blue, all the plaque that was slowly encrusting your teeth.

Beatrice staked her chin atop his head and made a totem pole. "*Hermano hermano hermano,*" she said. Calvin was learning Spanish at school; she was helping him.

"Loggia," he said indistinctly. He was still brushing his teeth.

"Aren't you finished yet?" Beatrice asked, leaning upon the sword just as a very tired and very bored old lady would rest upon her cane.

"Don't do that!" Calvin said, his mouth full of blue. He cherished his swords; he had three complete sets of armor and weaponry from three different periods of history. They were made of very durable plastic, but still: their mother had damaged the Roman-centurion one while trying to teach a lesson to the large raccoon that lurked about their driveway. Now, when brandished, it drooped in a pitiful way.

Beatrice turned on the bath. "Could I have a little privacy, please?" The bathtub was held up by four claws that looked as if they belonged to an eagle, or a big hawk. It was long enough so that you could submerge yourself entirely and still not feel anything pressing against your head or your feet. Beatrice and Calvin loved the bathtub. On Christmas they gave each other fat glass jars filled with bath beads, shining like jewels. Beatrice gave Calvin Peach Passion. Calvin gave Beatrice Gardenia. These she now deposited into the water. "I need to relax," she said.

"So do I," said Calvin mysteriously, as he retrieved his sword and floated out of the bathroom. The bathroom had two doors: one leading to his room, and the other to hers. In this way, it was like a joint. Beatrice turned off the lights. She stepped into her bath. "I'm in my bath!" she called out. She splashed about in the darkness, and then she was still. She felt everything around her: boughs brushing against square windows; the large raccoon lurking; a hawk skimming right over the roof. Things were astir, things she couldn't see. Out in the night, animals prowled and crept. Much farther away people were creeping about, too, making drug deals, going in and out of apartment buildings. The word, the idea—*apartment*—was enchanting. But she lived here, in the trees, at the very top of the house. Beneath her a gardenia bath bead dissolved, releasing its oil and its peculiar scent.

"IS ANYONE LISTENING? Anyone at all?" The radio spoke, glowing from her bookshelves.

Beatrice sat up in her bed. *She* was listening! In defiance of everyone: her mother and father, who fancied her asleep; her friends at school, who liked Prince and choreographed sexy dance routines to his songs; her piano teacher, for whom she played inventions and fugues, all the while thinking about an amplifier, a fuzzbox, a roadie. She didn't exactly know what all of these things were, but she wanted them. She knew they existed, because visitors to the Rock Hotel would mention them in conversation. There was a band, for instance, called We've Got a Fuzzbox and We're Gonna Use It, which was a mouthful, but that was the point. She was listening. She knew what to say. Not group: band. Not concert: show. You did not buy a ticket; you paid a cover at the door. Beatrice was paying attention, so that she would be prepared.

"Am I talking to myself?" the voice asked. "Am I the last person left?"

There was a long pause. "If you can hear me, I don't care who you are, you have to pick up the phone and call me. Now. Make a request. Win a prize. I don't care. You know what the number is."

Beatrice did in fact know the telephone number. She often practiced dialing it but never considered doing it for real. The DJ tended to criticize those who called up the Rock Hotel. His name was Shred. He would make fun of people's requests or else refer to them as psychopaths. "There are a lot of weird people out there," he would murmur. "And they all love to call me." But now he sounded lonely, and possibly like he was losing his mind. Beatrice wondered if she should reach out to him. Maybe in this vulnerable state he was less likely to belittle her.

She padded over to the radio and found the pocket diary she kept there, a gift from her mother, identical to those belonging to her brother and her father, in which they were each supposed to keep a growing list of Things to Do. In this diary Beatrice had written the names of the bands that she heard on the Rock Hotel: Squirrel Bait. Agent Orange. Pussy Galore. Angry Samoans. Big Black. Mission of Burma. The Cramps. She liked to copy these names in clean bold letters onto her school binders, and would be surprised to learn, at later points in her life, that these names were often attached to real things: *Samoa is a country? And Samoans are the people who live there?* They were islanders; they had been colonized; they had much to be angry about. But here, in the darkness and quiet of her bedroom, Samoans were simply residents of the Rock Hotel.

And as such, safe from ridicule. She would dial the number; she would ask for the Angry Samoans. It was safe. She told herself this as the line rang. But still her heart quickened, neatly, like the piano teacher's metronome, making her play the minor scales at increasingly reckless speeds. It was only a question of time before an accident occurred.

"Rock Hotel," a voice said.

"Shred?" Beatrice asked. "I'm listening!"

"Good to know," Shred said, sounding not at all close to the brink of despair. He sounded as if he were eating a sandwich. "What can I do for you?"

"Could you please play a song by the Angry Samoans?"

"Sure," Shred said. "Which song?"

She had no idea. In her pocket diary she had not yet begun writing down the names of songs. He said it so fast, all the information she needed to know.

"You choose," Beatrice said. "I trust you."

Shred made a swallowing noise. "Will do," he said. "Thanks for calling the Rock Hotel."

Beatrice put down the receiver. She felt damp all over. Standing in the dim light of the radio, she stroked the telephone. She stroked her pocket diary, and then the radio itself. He had been terribly kind to her. That's what she would say, if she ever met him—she *would* meet him, she decided, they would become friends and then go out together and live in an apartment—she'd say, "You were so nice! That first night we talked, you were so nice to me." She practiced saying it aloud. Then she practiced saying it in an English accent.

As she glided back to her bed, she stumbled upon something warm and human. She gasped, without wanting to, for she already knew who it was. "Calvin," she said. He was playing Cat Burglar.

She heard him slide into a sitting position; she heard him sigh with satisfaction. "That was a long time," he said. "Maybe a record." Though she couldn't see him, she knew what he was wearing: their mother's ancient turtleneck, the kind that was black and stretchy and had two long tongues that reached down and snapped together between the legs; black tights; black knitted gloves; a beret that their father had brought back from Montreal. The purpose of Cat Burglar was to slink into Beatrice's room without her noticing. Any burgling was incidental. Calvin had developed this game entirely on his own. For Beatrice, the most enjoyable aspect was suddenly switching on the light, because Calvin seemed to believe that making himself flat was the same as making himself invisible, and it was interesting to see him pressed into the floor, limbs spread, as if a cement roller had traveled over him, or else smushed against a wall, trying not to breathe.

She didn't turn on the light now. If she did, then all would be lost; she would see the flowers blooming on her bedspread; she would see the little porcelain lamp stand man leaning toward the lamp stand lady, his tiny porcelain lute in hand.

"Go to bed," she told Calvin. "You're feeling very, very sleepy."

"Who's English?" he wanted to know. "Who were you talking to?"

"Shred," she said, and despised herself for saying it. Her book jackets, her sweaters, her new pointy shoes, the toes already scuffed: she couldn't keep anything nice for longer than a minute. "He's not English."

"Who's Shred?"

"Shhhhhhhhhhhhhhh," Beatrice said, and moving her hands through the darkness, she found something shaped like Calvin. She guided it toward the door. In the radio's dim light, she saw the pair of sunglasses he had added to his disguise. These, combined with the beret, gave him the appearance of a strange and chic little person, like a boy whose parents are glamorous performers, and who spends his whole childhood drinking ginger ale in nightclubs. Beatrice filled with the intoxicating feeling of her brother being unfamiliar to her.

And then the radio spoke. It said, "This song goes out to the girl who wanted to hear some Angry Samoans."

"That's me," Beatrice whispered, to no one in particular.

Her other nighttime activity often enthralled her so completely that she would still be awake when Shred announced it was one o'clock in the morning. She would look up miserably at the lamp stand man casting his puny reflection against the black squares of her window. Having the light on in the middle of the night was a million times gloomier than having it off. But she needed the light to see what she was doing.

This other activity involved a pair of tweezers she had found in the first aid kit beneath the sink. In a slow but gratifying way, her eyebrows were disappearing. Everything else, meanwhile, was running amok. She seemed to have passed into another country, a place where it was impossible to remain intact: you found yourself shedding crooked snowflakes of skin, leaving squiggles of short, dark hair on your sheets. You were always leaving something behind. And it scared Beatrice, the thought that some excessive bit of her might detach itself and then be discovered by a tidier person. On a bar of soap, or in the collar of a sweater she had borrowed. The tweezers were not much help, in this unpleasant new country she had crossed into unawares; it would have been easier, maybe, to empty her bathtub with an eyedropper. But she kept them close at hand, inside the drawer of her bedside table, and at night she put them to furious use.

She was busy, but so was everyone else. They all had their projects. In the rooms below, her father was pushing furniture across the floor. Her mother was snapping rubber bands around handfuls of bobby pins, loose colored pencils, rolls of pennies. They opened and closed drawers. They raised and lowered their voices. They moved things around. And even Calvin was awake sometimes, splayed across the rug in his room, creating accord among his action figures. Beatrice could hear him murmuring, she could hear the chair legs scraping, she could feel the whole house ticking with their solitary habits, so it was no wonder then that in the mornings, her family, they did not look their best.

ONE NIGHT, LATE, THE telephone rang.

"Hello?" Beatrice said.

"Hey!" a voice said, sounding pleased. "How you doing?"

"Good," seemed the right way to respond. She said it again. "Good."

The person chuckled. "You don't know who this is."

"Sure I do!" Beatrice protested. "Of course I do. So how *are* you?"

"Happy to hear your voice."

"Well," she said. "I'm happy to hear yours."

He asked, "What are you doing right now?"

Beatrice dropped her tweezers onto the bedspread. "Nothing," she said. She tucked them back in their drawer. "Listening to the radio."

Her bed made a squeaking noise as she stood up, ready for the next question. He would ask, *Can I talk to your dad for a minute?* and she would pound down the four flights of stairs; she would get, on her way back, a Fruit Roll-Up from the kitchen. When the bed squeaked, she wondered, did it sound like she'd farted?

She waited for the question.

"That's funny. I'm listening to the radio, too."

"Oh."

"Maybe we have a psychic connection." And he chuckled again, to show that he was kidding.

As he said this, she realized that she did not, in fact, know the person she was speaking to. But it seemed too late to tell him that. And too late to feel alarmed. He was not an obscene phone caller, that much was for certain. She had received an obscene phone call before. Waiting for her brother on the steps outside the public library, she had heard the telephone ring from inside the telephone booth. When she answered it, a voice asked, Is your pussy very hairy? and though it would never have occurred to her to use those exact words, she did think to herself, as she slowly brought the phone down on the receiver, *How did you know?*

The person coughed on the other end of the line. "Excuse me," he said. "I'm getting over a cold."

The cough did not sound like it belonged to him. It sounded childlike and delicate and dry, like that of the rich little boy in *The Secret Garden*, who is wheeled about in a wicker chair with a blanket on his lap. He behaves peevishly until his better nature is revealed by someone poorer.

Beatrice said, "Bless you," as if the person on the telephone had sneezed.

"That's all right," he said. "Shouldn't you be in bed by now? Don't you have school in the morning?"

"No," she said, without irritation. For he hadn't asked in

a mindless way. And he wasn't looking for her father or her mother. Somehow she knew now he wasn't going to ask for them, ever.

"No," she repeated. "I'm not in school anymore." She closed her eyes to the bookshelves, and the pale blue bedside table.

She said, "I'm in a band."

"Like the Bangles?"

"No!" she shrieked; in embarrassment, in dangerous-feeling delight. He thought it was true. "Like the Butthole Surfers."

"Haven't heard of them," he murmured deferentially.

"They're obscure," she said. "A lot of people haven't."

This seemed a good time to mention her fuzzbox. Like a vocabulary word, she had to use it in a sentence: "I've got a fuzzbox" was all she could manage, which wouldn't have passed muster on a quiz at her school. But who was keeping score? She heard herself suddenly saying aloud a number of things that until then she had only been able to say silently, as an experiment in her head.

She also learned about a profession she hadn't known of before: landscaping. It involved the pruning and mowing of other people's yards. This was what he did, the person with the dainty cough on the other end of the phone. Her parents, she thought, could use a landscaper. Their own yard was wild and overgrown, and a great source of contention. Her father believed that lawns were not ecologically sound; her mother believed that this was an excuse. But Beatrice mentioned none of this. She had already created the impression that she no longer lived at home, and that she belonged to the kind of family who didn't even own a yard.

She detected something slithering across the floor. "Can you hold on a moment?" she asked, and clamped her hand over the mouth of the telephone.

"Calvin!" she said. "Please go burgle somewhere else!"

Something slithered away from her. Her bedroom door cracked open, and then it closed.

"Sorry," Beatrice said into the telephone.

"Can I ask you something?"

"Oh yes," she said.

"Who's that yelling?"

It was Beatrice's father. He was downstairs somewhere, thundering. Most likely the house was upsetting him. They had moved in more than three years before, but still their house hadn't ceased to surprise them: it flooded in the spring-time, ushered in hosts of flying ants, attracted the attentions of feral cats and raccoons. The chimney collapsed; the pipes burst; one windy afternoon, a red Spanish tile came flying off the roof and nearly hit Calvin on the head. The house was always in need of an expensive and immediate repair, the ac-cumulation of which had begun to deeply discourage their fa-ther. He seemed to have pictured repairs on a much smaller and more charming scale, repairs that could create camara-derie within a family. Everyone gathered together, genially refinishing a banister, not scores of heavy-booted workmen, clumping through the house like a marauding army. "This is not what I imagined!" their father would bellow, a sound both terrifying and wounded. It was a sound she imagined an elephant might make when captured, its trunk curling up to-ward the sky. But she couldn't figure out what he was saying now, with four long flights of stairs between them.

Beatrice took another chance. "It's my boyfriend," she said.

The person on the other end of the telephone paused.

"Should I hang up? Is he going to be mad?"

She pressed her mouth against the phone. "He already *is* mad."

"He is? What's he going to do?"

"I don't know," Beatrice whispered. "Wait—"

"What? What's that noise?"

From outside her door came a long and low-pitched hum, similar to the sound people make when they're cold: Brrrrrrrrrr.

"I think he's turned on the—" Beatrice inhaled sharply. "I have to go now."

She put the telephone back into its cradle. Click! And like that, he was gone. He had risen up from some unfathomable place, and now he had sunk back down again, like Champ, or the Loch Ness monster, about which Calvin was building a diorama. Beatrice herself felt waterlogged, as if she had stayed in the bath for too long.

Outside her door, the beautiful wooden box vibrated steadily. Calvin, in his extreme stealth, was probably pressed up against the little button in one of the rooms downstairs. Beatrice stretched out on her bed and listened to the bell hum, imagining herself a lazy servant. But she did so halfheartedly. According to the rules, she was never the servant. Just as she was never the pupil, but always the teacher; never the person who discovers the dead body, but always the body, lying cold and immobile on the floor. How did these rules come about? Although she had invented them, they made no sense to her; they were arbitrary yet inviolable. She knew, for instance, that the telephone would ring again, maybe not this night but another night, and that when it rang she would say, "Hello?" and that the rules would then take over: he asking her questions, and she dreamily offering answers. He would be a landscaper, and she would be a guitar player in a band.

Calvin came into her room, not slithering this time. She felt him breathing on her. "Why didn't you come?" he asked.

"Were you ringing for me?" Beatrice said.

"Yes!" Calvin said. "Why didn't you come?"

He turned on her bedside lamp and appeared, in his beret and sunglasses and gloves. Far beneath them, their father bellowed.

"Did the toilet explode again?" she asked.

Calvin frowned. "I don't know," he said finally. "I couldn't tell. I tried ringing you."

"I thought it was by accident," Beatrice said.

"I made it through the kitchen, with the lights on. They didn't see me. I snuck across the entire kitchen," Calvin said. "Then I snuck into the Butler's Pantry. I was waiting for you—I kept ringing the bell."

"I didn't understand," Beatrice said. "I thought you were pushing the button by mistake."

"Never mind," he said wearily. "Too late now."

He peeled off the black knit gloves and handed them to her. "You can have these back."

"Don't you need them?"

"No," Calvin said. "I don't. I'm done with that game."

Without his gloves, he didn't look like a cat burglar anymore. He didn't even look chic and international. He looked half dressed and forlorn in his turtleneck and tights, like a girl someone forgot to pick up after tap dancing class.

Now THAT HE HAD ABANDONED Cat Burglar, Calvin threw his energies into becoming a nosy person. It was as if all his passion for going undetected was now transformed into detecting something sneaky or amiss in Beatrice's life. He pestered her constantly. Standing outside the bathroom door, he would repeat, tonelessly: "What are you doing? What are you doing? What are you doing?"

Usually, Beatrice was practicing. Practicing lighting a cigarette, or driving a van and lighting a cigarette at the same time. Practicing talking with a cigarette dangling out the side of her mouth, or talking while gesturing with a cigarette in one hand. She had no cigarettes with which to practice, so she rolled up a little piece of paper and secured it with Scotch tape. Sometimes it was easier to use an invisible cigarette, like when she practiced sticking her cigarette between the tuning pegs of her guitar, which was also, at this point, invisible.

"What are you doing?" Calvin repeated.

"I'm smoking!" Beatrice shouted.

A moment of silence from outside the door. Then: "Beatrice . . . ," Calvin said in a threatening tone. And when she ignored him: "Beatrice . . . ?" he said, sounding afraid. "You shouldn't be smoking. You know you shouldn't be."

She flung the door open and glared. "I'm kidding. Ha ha. I'm only kidding."

Calvin also began taking an unhealthy interest in the Rock Hotel. "Is it on yet?" he would ask, hovering beside the radio. "Tell me when it's on," he ordered Beatrice. Anytime a voice came onto the air, even if it was only the weatherman, Calvin would say, "That's Shred, right? That's Shred." He pretended that he liked listening to the music, closing his eyes and nodding to the frenzied sounds. "I love that song," he'd say.

But Beatrice knew he was only pretending. For sometimes he would turn away from the radio, blink a few times, and ask musingly, "What are they so *angry* about?" He was still young enough to think in the same fretful ways as adults. In more charitable moods, Beatrice would say, "One day, Calvin, it will sound different to you." One day he would be able to tell, like she could, when a song was by Dag Nasty or Minor Threat, even before Shred said anything. "You will be able to tell the difference," she told him, "between being angry and being alive."

It was a distinction she tried to impart to the person on the telephone.

"Why is your boyfriend always yelling?" he asked.

"It's just what he does," she said. It had become what she did, too: shut her bedroom door and sing along to the Rock Hotel in a strained voice she didn't wholly recognize. *That's when I reach for my revolver!* she would yell, and it made her feel exhilarated, alert, terrifyingly capable. She couldn't wait until she could drive in a car and yell at the same time.

"Doesn't it bother you?"

"I don't take it personally," she said.

"Why don't you leave him?" the person asked. "Try someone new."

"You make it sound easy." She didn't like when the conversation sidled off in this direction. "When it isn't easy at all. Leaving is the hardest thing a person can do," she said firmly, and then reminded him: "We *live* together."

"I guess that's true," he admitted. "You get attached, I guess."

"And we'd have to break up the band."

"But you could start a new one. An all-girl band."

Beatrice sighed. "It's not that simple. I would still have feelings for him."

And she wondered at the ease with which she could talk about relationships, having never actually had one herself. It was amazing what practice and imagination could accomplish. By the time she went to her first show, moved into her first apartment, smoked her first cigarette, it would seem, she supposed, like she had been doing it for her entire life. Maybe by the time she had her first boyfriend, even, she would already be tired, having rehearsed so long for all of that trouble.

She explained, "Sometimes we don't have a say in who it is we love."

Even though she said it patiently, she had a feeling that he still didn't understand, and that he would persist in being obtuse when it came to this subject. There was a willful streak in him, a doggedness, as if he'd picked up the personality of a dandelion or a patch of crabgrass. He asked the same questions every time he called. He asked them in the same tentative, mournful tone. She was trying to break him of the habit.

"Tell me about your day," she demanded. "Tell me something interesting."

"Oh god," he moaned. He was stumped. "That's impossible."

Then, as if in disgust, the house shuddered. It was barely perceptible, no more than a mild spasm, because the house was so large and the walls so thick. Workmanship, she had heard repeated. Houses weren't made that way anymore. When someone slammed the back door, you hardly felt it.

There was the sound of metal scraping across the driveway, and then her father's voice, clear and deep and appalling: "I'm *doing* it!" he bellowed.

The person on the other end of the phone let out another moan.

"I don't get it," he muttered. "I don't get it at all."

How to explain?

"We have a lot in common," Beatrice said, and strangely, here in the hubbub of her inventions, was something true. Her father relished the tricky fugues she played for him. They both found the back of Calvin's neck irresistible to touch. And there was an abundance about him, an over-exuberance, that she was unhappily beginning to see in herself. When he hugged you, for instance, you could feel the springy growth beneath his shirt, and on the one hand it was revolting; on the other, it was like resting your cheek against moss.

"A lot in common," the person echoed, an idea that seemed at last to dishearten him, when obstacles such as the band, and the apartment, had allowed him hope. Maybe he felt, in all of his dullness, a knuckle of truth. He began to cough again in his childlike, enfeebled way.

But then he stopped coughing, so abruptly that it made seem as if he had been pretending all along. He spoke in a calm voice not unlike the one she used with him. He said, "What would you do if one day he just never came home?"

"Excuse me?"

"You'd be all alone. You'd want someone to hold you."

"I'm sorry?" she asked, as though his cough had prevented her from hearing him correctly. She decided that this cough made it impossible for her to hear much of what he said. His dry little cough was, she decided, settling farther into his chest; it was indicating quite ominous things about his health.

"You should take lozenges," she said briskly, suddenly ready to get off the telephone. *Lozenges* was a word she had acquired a year ago, during her book-reading era, before she had discovered the Rock Hotel, in the days when she was still planning to emigrate to England and become a historical novelist. How bizarre. That person, and the person she was now? They wouldn't even be friends.

THE TELEPHONE WASN'T ALWAYS in her room when she needed it. According to Calvin, he had calls to make. When she saw the long gray cord snaking out of her room and under his door, she would succumb, briefly, to bloodthirsty feelings. He had no one to talk to. Not at this hour. But she could hear him speaking in his bell-like voice, speaking slowly and precisely, like a person giving instructions to someone less intelligent. The conversations were always short. And always obviously pretend. She knew because she had done it herself, in the past, talk to the dial tone as though it were her closest friend.

It was all just an elaborate ruse to further him in his nosy pursuits. He always wanted to know whom Beatrice was speaking to. Whenever the telephone rang, he would dart into her room. "Is it for me?" he'd ask, though it never was. He simply needed an excuse to see who was calling.

Every one of Beatrice's answers he found unsatisfactory.

"Which guy?"

"Do I know him?"

"Does he go to your school?"

As for Beatrice, she couldn't decide which was harder: evading Calvin, or resisting the urge to tell him everything. She was frequently overwhelmed by a desire to flatten him with some shocking announcement. The sight of him checking for plaque, or sliding his trading cards into their plastic sleeves, or bobbing up and down to the Rock Hotel, filled her with a sort of mean-spirited abandon.

What would she tell him first?

Why 69 was a disgusting number. About a girl at her school who had slapped her own mother and knocked her glasses off. About girls who tortured other girls by cutting up magazines and sending them serial-killer letters. That Big Black's new record would be called *Songs About Fucking.* That she now knew what landscaping was. What DIY was; and PCP; and DOA.

Sometimes she wanted to descend on her brother like a

devastating angel and tell him every interesting thing she knew. But as it turned out, she didn't have to.

"A man called," Calvin said, holding the telephone. He stood in the doorway of Beatrice's bedroom. "Looking for you. I told him you weren't home."

"Why did you do that?" Beatrice asked, as she tugged the telephone away from him.

"He sounded funny," Calvin said. "He sounded like a creep."

"He's a friend," Beatrice said.

"That man?"

"We talk a lot on the phone."

"You do?" Calvin stared at her. "You talk to that man?"

"Stop saying that word!"

"What word?" he asked.

In her arms the telephone rang. She flinched, and put it down on her bed.

"Don't answer it," Calvin said.

"Of course I'm going to answer it. He's my friend, he's trying to reach me."

"Don't answer it. Don't talk to that—" But he wasn't allowed to say it.

The telephone kept ringing. She curled her fingers around the receiver.

"No!" Calvin said.

"There's nothing to worry about," Beatrice said, as she felt herself beginning to worry. "He's not at the front door. It's just the telephone."

"I know," Calvin said. "But please, don't answer it. I think it would be a bad idea."

He took her hands into his. They were hot and slightly

sticky. Together she and Calvin sat on her bed, watching the telephone ring. By the time it stopped, Beatrice felt afraid.

"Do you think . . . ," she began, and then couldn't finish the question.

If he appeared at their front door, she would not know him. Shred, she would know right away, by his beautiful long fingers and uncombed hair, the skeptical arch of his eyebrow, the leather cord he wore around his neck. But the person on the telephone had no face. He was neither straight nor stooped. His breath was not foul; his T-shirt was not clean or dirty; he had no birthmarks. He was neither nineteen nor forty-one. Without a harelip, a pierced ear; without a nose or a chin or a body. She did not wonder. She said only, "Hello." She said, "Tell me something interesting." He had a cough.

Her brother was looking at her in a peculiar way. His eyes moved over her face like it was a landscape and he was up in an airplane. His eyes said, *I am not coming down there.* But still they kept looking for a place to arrive.

Beatrice said, "He's not very smart."

"How do you know?"

"His job is mowing lawns," she said. "He didn't know what lozenges were. He believed it when I said I played guitar."

Calvin's eyes stood still.

"You believed he mows lawns."

She twitched.

Then she covered her ears and squeezed her lids shut. "Stop staring at me," she hissed. "Stop talking to me."

"Sorry," Calvin said, patting her arm. "Sorry."

Soft, tiny blows fell on her arms and her shoulders.

"Turn off all the lights," she told him. "Turn up the radio."

In the darkness, she opened her eyes. The radio was glow-ing. And Shred was still talking, announcing songs, disparag-ing requests, saying, "This one goes out to . . ."

"Maglite," Calvin whispered.

It was the most bludgeonlike thing either of them owned. The kind of flashlight that police officers and night watchmen used, the kind that required six enormous batteries, sliding down its cylinder with the cool weight of cannonballs. The Maglite lived inside Calvin's room, a universe she was no lon-ger so familiar with. She bumped into the umbrella stand that held his historic swords.

"Where are you, Calvin?"

He was crouching underneath the window. She reached out and touched his arm, and felt how he was cradling the flashlight. She acted like a blind person and touched him all over. He was still a citizen in that other country to which she had once belonged: all of a piece, flawless and moist, his chest lightly heaving like a hare's. From the other room the tele-phone rang once, and stopped.

"Oh god," Beatrice said. "Do you think they answered it?"

"I really hope not," her brother said, and from all around her, she felt the faintest draft seep in, as faint as someone blowing out a candle.

She thought of warning them. But here, on the very top floor of her house, there were no buttons embedded in the walls. Those buttons existed downstairs, in the rooms with the long windows, where her mother and her father lived. From here it was impossible to give warning, to say important things, to speak of danger; it was possible only to be summoned.

They would pick up the phone. They would answer the door.

"Oh god," she said.

Outside, something stirred. Something rustled through the trees and then stepped out onto the snow.

"Raccoon," Calvin whispered.

But it didn't sound like a raccoon, or a wild and mangy cat. It didn't sound like a hawk alighting on the lawn. She had once believed that she lived among the fir trees and the night-roaming animals, but now she remembered the street that wrapped around one side of their house, the scream of tires as they hit the hairpin curve; she remembered the gas station at the top of the hill, and the telephone booth beneath its buzzing lights. Beside her, her brother softly heaved. She could hear the crunch of footfalls on the snow.

Then Calvin shot up. He was too fast. He threw open the window, and the cold air came tumbling in on them.

"Stop! Don't move!" he cried.

"No!" Beatrice said, pulling on his leg. "Get down!"

"Kids?" a voice asked from below.

Beatrice stood up in surprise. Pressed against her brother, she peered out into the darkness. Calvin pushed the Maglite's tender black button, and a beam of light fell into the yard.

A man looked back up at them. He was protecting his eyes with one hand. In the other he held a bright blue duffel bag. He wore a long dress coat, pinned to the lapel of which was the unwieldy fir tree that Beatrice had made in her ceramics class a year before. She could see it even from here.

"Papa?" she said.

"What are you kids doing up?" their father asked, trying to sound mad and quiet at the same time.

"We heard something," Beatrice whispered back.

"What are *you* doing up?" Calvin wanted to know.

This question seemed to puzzle him. He dropped his hand to his side and lifted his duffel bag. "I was getting this from the car."

Calvin kept the beam of light trained on their father. "It's late!" Calvin said.

The light fell in a circle around him. Beyond that, Beatrice could make out the shape of trees rising up, and the untidy bushes, and the lopsided skeleton of the gazebo that he had begun building in the fall, but didn't have time to finish. She thought she spied something rotund in the darkness, loping toward the trash cans. She saw the marks her father's feet had left in the snow and the sharp shadow that his body threw onto the lawn. It was only her father. But something inside of her still clenched. It was only her father creeping about in the dark, and now he was standing there, holding his duffel bag, wearing her fir tree, his footsteps heading in one direction.

Tonight, she knew, he would go back inside. He would raise his voice, move furniture across the floor, and in the morning, around the table, the four of them would look into each other's tired faces. But one night, another night—soon, she thought—there would be an apartment.

And suddenly it was no longer her word, her idea.

"Calvin," she said. "Turn it off."

Without the flashlight, her brother wouldn't be able to see. She wrapped her hands around the cold cylinder and pulled.

But he did not let go. "No." He said fiercely, "It's late."

From behind her came the sound of the radio, speaking into the emptiness of her bedroom. The voice said, "This kid who keeps calling me, he wants to hear the Clash. Now normally, I would never play the Clash. Yes, I know, we wouldn't have punk rock without them, but I mean, you can hear the Clash on other radio stations. You can hear the Clash on *oldies* stations. We just don't play the Clash here on the Rock Hotel," Shred explained. "But this kid who called, he got me thinking about when I was his age, when I heard the Clash for the first time. I had never heard anything like them. *London Calling*— that record changed me. I wouldn't be sitting here talking to you if it wasn't for that record. So I'm going to play that song, for that kid who called. What can I say? It's a song of my youth."

Crossing

MR. MEACHAM, THE DEPARTMENT chair, offered to buy Ms. Hempel a lemonade after school. If you are a person of passion and curiosity and ferocious intellect, he told her, you are a born history teacher.

"I teach English," Ms. Hempel said.

"You don't teach English," Mr. Meacham corrected her. "You teach reading, and writing, and critical thinking!"

It seemed, to Ms. Hempel, a grand way of putting it. Through the wide café windows, she watched her students come barreling out of the school's front gates. Did she really teach them anything? Or was she, as she often suspected, just another line of defense in the daily eight-hour effort to contain them.

"What's wrong with the way history is taught in this school?" Mr. Meacham asked.

"Not relevant to the kids?" Ms. Hempel ventured.

"Relevant!" he cried. "Whoever said history had to be relevant?"

He then spoke in a pinched, miserable voice that Ms. Hempel had never heard before. "Look, kids, the ancient Egyptians aren't so different from us after all! Look, kids, when we study the ancient Egyptians, we're studying a reflection of ourselves!

"All this fuss about relevance," he said, restored to normal, "is a process of erosion. There won't be any history left by the time they're through. Just *social studies*." And Mr. Meacham leaned back on his stool, nervously, as if he were History and Ms. Hempel were Relevance.

"When students look at history," he said, "they shouldn't see their own faces; they should see something unfamiliar staring back at them. They should see something utterly strange."

But that's what they do see when they look in the mirror, Ms. Hempel thought. Something strange.

"So, no, that's not what I had in mind," Mr. Meacham continued, somewhat more cheerfully. "I'll tell you what's wrong with the way history is taught in this school: not enough writing. A lot of reading, a lot of talking, but not much writing. And that"—Mr. Meacham smiled at Ms. Hempel—"is where you can help."

"Me?" Ms. Hempel asked.

"You can teach them. Not only how to think about history, but how to write about it."

Ms. Hempel saw that Mr. Meacham was mistaken. He had confused her with someone who *liked* teaching seventh graders how to write, who felt happiest and most useful when diagramming a sentence or mapping an idea or brightly suggesting another draft. This was not the case. The thought of increased exposure to seventh-grade writing made Ms. Hempel worry. What happened when one read too many Topic Sentences? Already she could feel how her imagination had begun to thicken and stink, like a scummy pond.

If only she could develop for her subject the same dogged affection that Mr. Meacham felt for his. People approached her, possessed by their enthusiasms, and Ms. Hempel would think, How beautiful! She loved enthusiasm, in nearly all its forms. For this reason she found herself scorekeeper for the volleyball team, facilitator for the girls-only book group, faculty adviser to the Upper School multicultural organization, Umoja. And now, teacher of seventh-grade United States history.

Mr. Meacham handed her a book that weighed approximately ten pounds. Its title, she noted, was full of enthusiasm (*America! America!*).

FIRST ASSIGNMENT. CHOOSE three people, of different ages (in other words, don't grab the three seventh graders sitting closest to you), and ask them the following question: Why is it important to learn about American history? Record your findings. Include the name, age, and occupation of your interview subjects. Bring in your results and share them with the class.

"'To help us better understand ourselves,'" Tim read from his binder. "Alice Appold. Forty-two. Chiropractor."

"I didn't know your mom was older than mine," Daniel said.

"My mom is fifty-three!" Rachel announced with dismay.

"Ms. Cruz said that the reason it's important to know about American history is because if we don't know our past, then we don't know our future." That was Stevie.

"My father said he won't answer the question because it's leading," Kirsten said.

"'It's our responsibility as citizens,'" Tim read, again from his binder. "James Appold. Forty-three. Restaurateur."

"My mother said that if we don't understand the struggles our ancestors went through, we won't appreciate the nice life that we have now," said Sophie, staring at Tim, who hadn't raised his hand.

Julia Rizzo spoke next. "'Those who don't remember the past are condemned to repeat it.'"

Six students looked up in territorial surprise.

"That's what my mother said!"

"So did mine!"

"I was just about to say that."

"My sister," said the other Julia, who would never have the same answer as anyone else, "told me that not knowing your history is like being a person who's lost their memory."

"An amnesiac," Kirsten said bossily.

Amnesiac, Ms. Hempel wrote on the board, and then experienced an instance of it herself. It was a condition that sometimes afflicted her. She would turn her back to the class; she would forget everything. What *is* a noun? Who *were* the Pilgrims? And, more troubling, What was I saying? Or: How did I get here? The tether would snap, and she would be set adrift, the sleek green board stretching out all around her. She would feel, against her back, the warmth of eighteen faces. She would feel she might do anything in this moment, like sing a song from *My Fair Lady*. But then a pigeon departs from the windowsill, Stevie lets out a hiccup, a telephone, somewhere in the building, rings; and she recovers. Oh yes. I am Ms. Hempel. It is second period. A noun is a person, place, thing, or idea.

"A person who's lost her memory," Ms. Hempel said to the other Julia. "How true."

And she thought of the terrible blank she had drawn the very day she'd been hired to teach at this school. Upon signing her contracts and shaking everyone's hand, she found herself sitting in the faculty lunchroom over a plate of garbanzo bean salad and across the table from Mr. Meacham, who, as it turned out, taught a course in Chinese history. He was disappointed to learn that she did not speak the language, not a word of it.

"And your family?" he had asked. "What province are they from?"

It was at this point that Ms. Hempel's memory failed her. Hunan? Szechuan? Were those provinces or just restaurants? And what kind of food was she, by hereditary right, supposed to most enjoy? She knew the answer, she did! She was simply nervous.

"Chungking?" she murmured, which didn't sound particularly correct, but Mr. Meacham was already moving on.

"What a shame," he said, "that your name isn't more indicative."

"Yes." She didn't understand what he meant. "It is too bad."

"Is there a middle name, perhaps?"

"Grace?"

Mr. Meacham frowned, thinking. "Or a family name. Your mother's maiden name?"

"It's Ho."

"Ah!" He smiled and swallowed the last of his milk. "Have you ever thought of hyphenating?"

He tried it out. He used the word *euphonious*. He said the name over to himself, three times.

"Ms. Ho-Hempel," she said. "That's what they would call me?"

Mr. Meacham nodded happily.

"But—" How could she put this? "Won't there be a lot of jokes?"

He didn't follow.

"You know, *ho*? As in, 'pimps and.' As in, 'you blankety blank—'" She waved her hands at Mr. Meacham, as if guiding him into a very tight parking space. "Do I want a bunch of seventh graders calling me *ho*?"

Mr. Meacham looked at her, perplexed. "That's precisely the idea."

He picked up his lunch tray. "You'll be expanding their horizons. An awful phrase, but a sound principle."

She had a whole summer to practice saying it. Ho-Hempel. She even wrote it down on her name tag for the new faculty orientation. But when the first day of school finally arrived, children came crashing into her homeroom and by the time the last of them appeared—Michael Reggiano, congenitally late—she had lost her resolve altogether.

Ms. HEMPEL LIKED THE land bridge theory, especially the part about the lumbering mammoths and the hunters in hungry pursuit. The hunters were following the game, a phrase that made her think of small boys running after ducks in the park. The two things couldn't be at all similar; following the game was probably a lengthy and thankless process involving mammoth dung and very little real chasing or spear throwing. But still, that was how she pictured it: the band of hungry hunters pursuing a herd of lumbering mammoths. These hunters were so absorbed by the chase, they went running across a land bridge connecting their home, Asia, to an entirely unfamiliar and uninhabited continent, North America, without even noticing it. A land bridge was more difficult to imagine. The book described ice ages, glaciers, the freezing of oceans, their bottoms now exposed. Did that make sense? Did that big glacier, pinned atop the world like a yarmulke, somehow suck up the water in the Bering Strait? Apparently so. In that case, was crossing the land bridge like skirting a rampart of ice, the cold blue glacier bearing down on you from one side, or was it like trudging along a marshy strip of beach, with the glacier a white ship floating off in the distance? The book didn't elaborate. All that mattered was the appearance of the land bridge, so that the mammoths could lumber across, so that the Asian hunters could follow, so that the Western Hemisphere could become populated.

"Any questions?" Ms. Hempel asked.

"WHAT IF FERDINAND AND ISABELLA hadn't given Columbus the money?" asked Travis, who enjoyed hypothetical situations.

"What if the hunters hadn't crossed the Bering Strait?" he would eventually ask.

And, "What if the Pilgrims had decided to stay in Holland?"

Ms. Hempel wasn't sure how to answer these questions.

"Then I guess we wouldn't be sitting here!" she would reply, airily.

This seemed to be the answer Travis was looking for. He nodded and said, "I guess not."

GRANDPA'S CHEST. *THE YEAR IS 1691, and the settlers at Jamestown are packing up and moving the colony inland. Imagine that you are helping your grandfather sort through his belongings. Each item that he puts into his chest reminds him of some significant event or person in Jamestown's history. For instance, an old tobacco pouch might remind him of the crop that saved the colony from total ruin ("Ah, I remember it well—if Pocahontas hadn't taught John Smith how to plant tobacco, we never would have survived. But rich folk back home loved chewing the stuff. Soon everybody was growing it—even in the streets!"). Write a scene in which you describe this conversation with your grandfather as he reminisces over the contents of his chest. Note: You will need to include at least eight items!*

"Before I read my scene," Audrey said, "can I tell a joke?"

Ms. Hempel said yes.

"My father told it to me. It's a dumb joke, but I wanted to tell it. First he said, 'Why is it important to learn about American history?' Remember? The assignment we did? And then he said, 'Those who don't remember the past are condemned to repeat'"—Audrey paused, sheepishly—"'the seventh grade!'"

The class laughed. So did Ms. Hempel.

"The best reason yet!" Ms. Hempel declared. "Who wants to repeat the seventh grade?"

And then it occurred to her: *She* was repeating the seventh grade, in fact for the fourth time, and she would still be repeating the seventh grade when Audrey and Kirsten and Travis were out in the world, doing things. Over and over again, the Jamestown settlers would complain of the mosquitoes, the tea chests would tumble into the harbor, the Loyalists would be tarred and feathered and paraded through the crooked streets. Every November, the war would be won; every October, the colonies would rebel; every September, Ms. Hempel would turn to the board, pick up the chalk, and write: *First Assignment.*

OUT OF ALL THE DAYS in the month, Affinity Day was perhaps the most difficult. Ms. Hempel questioned the choice of *Affinity*, which she normally used to describe how she felt about Thomas Hardy, but the word was already a fixture, Umoja's gentle way of saying No White People Allowed. The organization's founders had decided, in the interests of unity, that once a month its nonwhite members should congregate without its white members. Or, to put it a preferable way, its members of color should gather without its members of noncolor.

Now Ms. Hempel was left with a classroom half full of students, nervously rattling their lunch trays. Where to begin? The white members probably suspected that as soon as the door swung shut, the Korean kids would start speaking Korean, and the Puerto Rican kids would start speaking Spanish, and the black kids would start speaking in some new and alluring way that no one else had caught up to yet. From inside the room would come the sounds of profound relief: laughter, slapping of hands, little moans of commiseration. Delicious food would be shared. Maybe some hilarious imitations of the other, absent members would be performed.

"So," Ms. Hempel began. "Is there anything that's on your mind? Anything you'd like to talk about?"

Everyone concentrated on their lunches. No one wanted to talk. The wall clock suffered one of its attacks; the minute hand shot forward, and then jumped back again. Balancing their trays, they had come, docile and curious and considerate of Ms. Hempel, but they didn't know what to do next. She didn't know how to show them. She exhaled noisily to signal that it was now safe to let go, but no one seemed to take her cue. Perhaps they weren't holding in their breaths.

Perhaps they moved through this school with ease and ownership; perhaps it was unfair to expect that they should feel discomfort. But that's what Ms. Hempel half hoped would come spilling forth: tales of woe, a collection of slights and insults and misunderstandings. Wonderment at the nature of one's hair; clumsy impressions of the deli man's accent. Expectations of brilliant athleticism, or of preternatural skill with calculations. A belittling of one's dearest accomplishments: *We all know why* she *got in early to Yale.* They could gather together here, with their lunch trays, and share these offenses. Theirs would be a kinship based on grievance. Then Ms. Hempel could feel as if she were providing something: a community; a sense of—affinity.

But no one was talking. Either they felt no outrage, no struggle or unease, or else they felt all these things and were not comfortable enough around Ms. Hempel, or each other, to describe it. Ms. Hempel feared that the latter was true—for she was aware of the struggle, she had been witness to it—she had seen Alex and Corissa and Andréa walking toward the bus stop, their heads bent together in solace and conspiracy; she had seen Nestor smiling, widely, entreatingly, altogether too readily; she had seen Clive rambling down the hallway, looking as if he had lost something. It could not be easy, being at this school. She had no way of fortifying them. In fact, she was making it worse—making them trail up here to her classroom, making them parade out of the lunchroom, carrying their trays.

Ms. Hempel felt the tenuousness of her claim. She wished she wasn't only half.

"Well, I have something on my mind," said Amara, Umoja's newly elected president. "I had an encounter with Mr. Meacham."

It concerned the list of research topics that he had presented to his Intellectual History class. "According to Mr. Meacham, Montaigne and Hobbes and Ralph Waldo Emerson were the only ones around doing any thinking."

Amara spoke of the great Nubian civilization, its delicate art and extensive trade and ingenious devices for irrigating the land. And the kingdom of Aksum—their alphabet and their gods, the grandeur of their obelisks! The stone thrones and colossal statues. She then leapt over thousands of years, arriving at Wole Soyinka and Léopold Senghor and Chinua Achebe. Glorious thinkers, all of them.

Amara remembered Ms. Hempel. "Look at the Chinese!" she added. "They had poetry, and philosophy, gunpowder and noodles and silk, when all those Europeans were running about waving clubs at each other. Wearing animal pelts!"

THIS WAS A WAY OF THINKING that Ms. Hempel couldn't quite rid herself of. As she accompanied her class through the Reformation, and the growth of European empires, and the race to explore, and the discovery of the new continent, and the settlement of the first English colonies, she often found herself wondering, What was going on in the rest of the world? Her thoughts would begin, Meanwhile, back in China . . . but she wasn't sure how to finish the sentence.

All that she could say for certain was that the English colonists seemed an unhygienic, scrabbling bunch. They died off at an alarming rate.

"Does that mean that we're going to see people dying?" asked Jonah.

"Possibly," Ms. Hempel said. "But if anyone dies, remember that it's a re-creation."

"It will look real, though," Jonah said. "Won't it?"

It should, if Plimoth Plantation recreated death with the same devotion with which it clothed its inhabitants, bred their livestock, built their dark and smoky homes. Ms. Hempel had studied the brochure. Upon any day of the week, one could step back into the year 1627. Scores of thrifty colonists would mill about you, busy with their chores: cleaning muskets, plucking chickens. And when you asked them a question—Why did you come to America? Or, What is that there you're growing?—

the colonists would look up mildly from their labor, and offer you an off-the-cuff and fascinating answer. They might then introduce themselves: Captain Standish, Goody Billington, Governor Bradford. Each colonist's accent was true to the English county from which he or she hailed. Even the swine were recreated: modern pigs, being too dainty, had been crossbred with a warthog; thus the hairy, truculent animals that now rooted about at the edges of the settlement. Ms. Hempel was very excited to see it all for herself, even though it did mean spending a long time on a bus.

"Ask lots of questions!" she yelled, trying to secure the seventh grade's attention. The bus was luxurious, its seats high-backed and plush. Probably every kind of mischief was occurring, unseen. "You will get the most out of the experience that way!"

Ms. Hempel worried that her students might be overawed by the colonists, might spend the whole day staring at the strange pigs. So she had assembled a list of suggested questions, of the type that curious seventh graders might ask an English colonist. These she distributed as the kids came careening down the aisle of the bus, tangled up in their backpacks and clipboards and sweaters. Ms. Burnes waited outside to make sure they didn't go anywhere.

Ms. Hempel stepped off the bus last. The air! It delighted her, it was brisk and wood-smoky; it smelled the way early music sounded: thin, feverish, slightly out of tune. Ms. Hempel hurried to the top of the path, flapping her hands to encourage the seventh graders, who tended to clot and clump and meander off into the distance; she touched their arms, she called to them, "Just a bit farther! Just over the crest of that hill!" And there it was: the settlement, the colonists, the sea. The blue sky, and the white smoke rising up in wispy streams. The roofs, gray and matted; the gardens, brown and stumpy; the roosters, red-crowned and wandering. The fort, with its cannons peeking out from under its eaves. The high, ragged fence, running along the perimeter of the settlement. Its purpose was to protect the colonists at night—to keep out the Spanish, or unfriendly Indians, or wild, hungry creatures of the forest.

"But you don't sleep here, do you?" Jonah wanted to know. "After this place closes, you go home."

The colonist scratched at his delicate beard. "Aye, I go home and sleep in my own bed. You can see it yonder," he said, pointing at a grey roof. "And if you happen upon my wife, you tell her that I will be back for the midday meal."

About eight or so seventh graders had another colonist surrounded. He was leaning jauntily upon an axe.

"What was the voyage over like?"

"What was your profession in England before you came here?"

"Did you come here for religious freedom or economic opportunity?"

"How do you feel about King Charles marrying a Catholic?"

"What is the literacy rate in the colony?"

They looked up from their sheets and stood braced for his answers, their clipboards jutting forward. Soon they would be free to climb on things and poke long, tough blades of grass into the animals' pens. But the colonist, suddenly, had turned gruff. "I was a planter there, in England, and I am a planter here," he said, before wielding his axe and letting it fall decisively into an upended log. The seventh graders moved away, in search of a more obliging colonist, and Ms. Hempel followed, whispering, "Have *conversations* with them."

But some children needed no prompting. Peering into the

dim interiors of the houses, Ms. Hempel saw Annie explaining, with many violent shakes of her pencil, why Indians ought not to be called savages; Daniel squatting beside the fireplace, examining the contents of a big, tarnished pot; Maria reaching out and stroking a woman's dress, asking, is it scratchy? Does it itch?

Jonah was looking around for the dying. He couldn't even find a colonist who was feeling sick. He ran up to Ms. Hempel and told her this, rather pointedly.

"It isn't winter yet," Ms. Hempel said. "Come back a few months from now, and they'll be dropping like flies."

She drifted about the settlement blissfully. She ran her fingertips along the fence; she pressed her nose into the marigolds that hung drying from the ceilings. She asked, in every house she entered, what was cooking for supper. The seventh graders darted about her, but they seemed, to her enchanted eye, nearly invisible: a school of silver minnows, and she, a great, stately carp. All she saw were the marigolds drying, and the bread rising in the wooden trestles, and the colonists calling to each other from their chores. Ms. Hempel surrendered, without protest.

"So where are all the kids?" Jonah was asking Governor Bradford. "Why aren't there any kids around?"

"Why, the lambing season does not come until spring!" said Governor Bradford. "You will not find any kids before April."

"Children," Jonah said. "You know what I mean. There aren't any children here. Because they're all at school."

"Nay, we have neither school nor schoolmaster here, but we hope for a schoolmaster soon to come from England."

"Their real school," Jonah said. "They can't skip it. That's why they aren't here."

"Have you not seen our children?" Governor Bradford asked. "Mine own son was here not a moment ago. He went to fetch wood for the fire. And Winslow's two girls wished me a good afternoon, but a minute afore you spake to me. They were on their way to gather crab apples, it being the season to harvest them."

"Very convenient," said Jonah.

"If you do not see our youngfolk, it is because they must work. No one rests here," said Governor Bradford, with finality.

How magnificent! Ms. Hempel rejoiced. How unperturbed he was, how convinced. Governor Bradford was unmistakably himself. Ms. Hempel aspired to such a performance. If only she, too, were a colonist. But why not? She could learn to do these things: to sew a jerkin, render fat into soap, and muck out a barn. She could say aye, and betwixt, and if the Lord wills it so. As she herded the seventh grade back onto the bus, and frowned at the little wooden muskets they had purchased at the gift shop, and reminded them to put their notes in a very safe place, she entertained the possibility. When she returned home, she would write a letter to the Plantation. Of course, she could not ask a colonist how she might join them; they would rebuff her, good-naturedly, just as Governor Bradford had done with Jonah. She must address her letter to the administration, who were probably tucked away somewhere behind the bluffs. Perhaps a whole network of cubicles and fluorescent lights stretched out beneath the settlement, hidden and labyrinthine. Her letter would be opened by one of these underground workers; a response would be posted; by next fall, she could be bending over, stoking a fire, and when the seventh grade came tumbling through, she would glance up; she would say, "My name is Alice Bradford, and aye, the voyage over was a dreadful one."

THE CHILDREN RUSTLED AND murmured in their seats; Ms. Hempel and Ms. Burnes had repossessed all of the muskets, which, as it turned out, fired rubber bands; the bus hummed along the highway. Ms. Hempel dozed against the window, and thought of Plimoth. But the more clearly she imagined herself there, the more she longed to be somewhere else. Somewhere the flies didn't cluster above the food, somewhere the dresses didn't itch. Somewhere she didn't have to spend all Sunday upon an uncomfortable bench, listening to sermons. She wanted to be somewhere clean, and civilized, and sweet-smelling, where everything she touched pleased her finger-tips. She wanted to be . . . in China!

If, in Plimoth, she rises before the dawn, and lugs water from the icy stream, the bucket bumping against her, then, in China, she wakes to the sound of bells tinkling in a breeze, and the patter of tiny footsteps racing across the courtyard, the plash of a fountain, and a merry child laughing. The floor is cool beneath her feet; the robe slides over her, like liquid. She has slept for many hours, and dreamt of landscapes, of journeys, of an old man living on the very top of a mountain. She will go out into the garden and her father will interpret her dreams.

If, in Plimoth, her garden is wild with tansy and mugwort and raggedy spearmint, then, in China, her garden is one of peonies, and tea roses, and lychee trees, and chrysanthemums. It is a garden of craggy rock and still water; in the pool grows a forest of lotus blossoms. Her father sits beneath the pavilion, his eyes closed lightly in thought. Sunlight stipples his lap; a butterfly alights there; a cicada chirrs by the still waters of the pool. "Father," she calls to him, "tell me the meaning of my dream."

"You must write a poem," he says, and he summons the ink boy. A rosy child appears, round and soft as a peach, bearing the bamboo brushes, and the inkstone, and a scroll of strong, translucent paper. He lays the inkstone upon the ground; it is smooth and dark, coolness rising from its surface like a mist, and with quick, sure strokes, the ink boy grinds the cake. Upon the inkstone there appears another pool, black and still, a perfect miniature of the pool beside which the ink boy sits and grinds. He will continue grinding as she writes, so that the pool will never shrink, so that the flow will not be interrupted once inspiration takes hold of her.

Her father is pleased with the poem. "You found the meaning of your dream," he tells her, and he reaches inside his robe. When his hand reappears, it is holding a peach. She takes it from him, and sees that it is not a peach, that though it is round and pleasing as the boy, it is smooth and hard as an inkstone. It is ivory, carved in the likeness of a peach. Upon looking very closely, she sees that tiny ivory monkeys are clambering up its cheek. One balances precariously atop the stem, its monkey arm outstretched in invitation. Upon looking even more closely, she sees that the top of the peach can be removed, like the lid of a teapot, and that the monkey is inviting her to open it. Off comes the top of the peach, and she is delighted to discover that attached to its underside is a delicate ivory chain, and that attached to the chain are more monkeys, hanging off wildly, in attitudes of rascality and abandon. It is as if, inside the peach, every kind of mischief is occurring, unseen. But there are not only monkeys dangling off the delicate chain, there are also treasure boxes, and pods. The treasure boxes are carved shut, but the pods, she finds, can be opened with the help of a thumbnail. Inside the pods? Tiny monkey babies, curled up in sleep. Each successive pod is tinier than the last; each monkey baby more perilously small. She eases the chain, the monkeys, the pods, back inside the peach. She replaces the top. She is filled with the delicious, dangerous sense that if she were to continue extracting the chain, the pods would grow even smaller, as would the monkeys and the treasure boxes and the very links of the chain itself, smaller and smaller, until they all but disappeared. "Thank you, Father," she says, and slips the peach deep inside her robes, where it will be safe.

Above her rises a face, smooth and round like a moon, or a peach, or the seed of a lychee nut. Two eyes gaze at her, black and still like a pool.

"Ms. Hempel." It is Jonah. His chin is resting atop a high, plush seat. His dark eyes shine in the light from a streetlamp outside the bus. "We're home," he says. "Wake up."

Ms. Hempel stirs. "I'm awake," she says. And she is; her eyes are open.

"I thought that place was fun," Jonah says.

"So did I," she says, and suddenly wants to reach up, to touch him on his cheek.

Ms. Hempel had told her class about the Indians' admirable habits. "Even the hooves," she said, "would be used as ceremonial rattles." She drew a circle on the chalkboard to illustrate the wholeness of their lives, and inside of this she wrote the words *harmony* and *balance*. When she described the Europeans' profligacy, and their brutal massacres, her students became enraged, and when she described the shrinking of the Indian population, they looked bereft. "But there's a silver lining," Ms. Hempel said. "I guess you could call it that."

Then she told them about the casino she had visited the previous summer: the great glittering elevators, the famous comedian, the tables thronged with customers, all losing money. "The Pequots are very rich and powerful now," she said, and the class grinned with relief.

Having spoken of the Indians so approvingly, Ms. Hempel was dismayed to find, during a Sunday afternoon in the bookstore, a new publication dedicated to contradicting her. She stood in the aisle and frowned. According to the latest anthropological discoveries, Indians were not good friends to Nature; they clear-cut forests, hunted game to near extinction, savored delicacies such as the buffalo fetus while leaving the mother to slowly decompose in the sun.

The book was displayed on a shelf that held a variety of other books all with apparently the same bent. Ms. Hempel realized that a small industry had sprung up, whose sole purpose was to reveal the lies and hoaxes of American history. Paul Revere did not shout "The British are coming!" Thomas Jefferson did seduce and impregnate Sally Hemings, his slave. The founding fathers were not in the least bit interested in equality for all. And mad John Brown was perfectly sane. Even the land bridge theory was under attack. It looked like the first Americans didn't wander over the Bering Strait, after all.

Ms. Hempel felt irritated and betrayed. It had taken her a long time to finish reading *America! America!*, and now here was a whole shelf of scholarship casting doubt on everything that she was about to teach.

But—she admitted it—these books did seem necessary; their existence made sense to her. History was so difficult to tell truthfully. A person could not be relied upon to faithfully recount her own past, much less the story of an entire country.

Before she discovered the history section, she had sat in a very comfortable chair, looking at a book of stories. The story she happened to read concerned a girl visiting boarding schools with her parents. At one of the schools, the campus is divided in half by a public street, and students must cross the street between classes. That night, the girl tells her parents that she likes this school best; she is impressed by how the students saunter across the street without even checking to see if there is traffic coming.

As she read the passage, Ms. Hempel trembled with recognition. It was her school! Not the school she taught at, but *her* school, the one she had gone to as a student. It had to be— the ancient campus, the street, the students ambling across. And, as whenever she thought of her school, Ms. Hempel was overcome by affection and wistfulness. What a magical time that was, how wonderful! She had spent four years there, in all seasons, but whenever she pictured her school, it was always late afternoon, and the light was always golden, the treetops always red; a boy sat cross-legged on the quad, and a guitar was in his lap. Somewhere, a pile of leaves was burning.

These feelings were very powerful, and they were also patently untrue. Ms. Hempel understood, quite rationally, that she had spent her four years in a state of fury and bewilderment. She had never understood how a person could be coltish until she saw the girls at her school—awkward, blond, impossibly appealing, chasing after soccer balls and hockey pucks and lacrosse balls with a long, loping stride and furious concentration. She gained weight in protest. She hid out in the costume closet, drinking cough syrup and despising the Grateful Dead. She won the role of a blowsy prostitute in the school play. When her history teacher, Mr. Warren, looked to her hopefully during a discussion of immigration, she scowled. Typical, she thought. She wrote a poem about it.

And if she didn't look when she crossed the street, it was because she was too preoccupied, thinking of ways she might shock or demolish her school.

There had to be a sort of dangerous magic at work—when she was a student, she never felt, for even a day, that the school belonged to her, or she to it; and now here she was, sitting in a bookstore, recognizing herself as one of those blessed, oblivious, coltish people who could cross a public street without looking both ways. She had read the story; she had thought, My school! But it probably wasn't her school; there were probably at least a hundred other schools just like it, schools where students believed that if they sauntered out into the street, traffic would stop for them. Now she was inducted into that awful confederacy.

SHE HAD SCOWLED AT MR. WARREN, her history teacher, but even if she had decided to join the discussion, she wouldn't have had much to say. Her mother remembered little about the crossing. She was six years old at the time; all she could distinctly recall were the boys, diving for coins. The boat had anchored in Hawaii, and the passengers had stood along the railing, mesmerized—or so Ms. Hempel imagined—by the harbor and the people and all the activity. For days they had seen nothing but water. The most charming attraction was the boys, balanced along the edge of the pier like birds. If you tossed a coin over the railing, the boys would tip over into the water, easy as you please, as if tumbling into sleep. Straight down they dove, until they disappeared. The passengers would lean over the railing, peering breathlessly below them. And then a sudden rushing, a breaking of the surface, and a single arm appears, a beaming face, a hand holding up a bright coin for everyone to see. The boys paddle back to the pier, hoist themselves up, resettle; they turn their faces to the boat.

"Your grandmother remembers it all much more clearly than I do," her mother had said. "You should ask her about it." And, although she should have known that to suggest the idea would be to instantly sabotage it, she added, "You could interview her, use a tape recorder. You could do an oral history project."

Ms. Hempel had planned to ask her grandmother; in good moods, she had even considered the project her mother suggested. She had also planned to learn Mandarin once she reached college. She did still plan to learn it; she did still mean to ask her mother about the objects illuminated inside the case at the far end of the living room: an inkstone; a brush; a peach, carved with monkeys; a scroll.

Yurt

A YEAR AGO Ms. DUFFY HAD come very close to losing it, with her homeroom right next to the construction site for the new computer lab, and her thwarted attempts to excise the Aztecs from the fifth-grade curriculum, and her ill-fated attraction to Mr. Polidori. But now, upon her return, she looked unrecognizably happy. She held court in the faculty lounge, her hair longer than ever, her big belly sitting staunchly on her lap and demanding rapt attention from everyone but her. Above the belly, Ms. Duffy laughed and swayed and acted careless with her hands, as if to say, Why, this old thing?

Ms. Hempel couldn't take her eyes off it. It looked as tough as a gourd.

"Yemen is magical," Ms. Duffy was saying. "Just unbelievable. The pictures—the pictures don't capture it at all."

A stack of parched-looking photographs circulated around the lounge. After her difficult year, Ms. Duffy had sublet her apartment and struck out for the ancient world. At first, her e-mails had been long and poetical and reasonably free of gloating, though full of figs, marketplaces, bare feet against cool tiles, shuttered naps at noon. In between classes Ms. Hempel would stand in front of the faculty bulletin board and read about Ms. Duffy's naps, trying to detect in these messages a note of melancholy, of homesickness. *Miss you all!!* Ms. Duffy would write in closing, but the absence of a subject, as well as the excessive punctuation, made the sentiment seem less heartfelt. And then the e-mails stopped arriving altogether.

Ms. Hempel studied the photograph that had been passed to her: a blazingly bright and empty street with the tiny figure of Ms. Duffy standing at its center. Who had taken the picture—a Yemenese friend? A Yemenan? Both sounded lovely, though incorrect. It seemed important to know who had stood in the shade of those massive, intricate buildings and held the camera. Perhaps this was the first of many foreign transactions that would result, so spectacularly, in Ms. Duffy's new belly.

Ms. Hempel waved the photograph in the air. "Anna, where was this one taken?"

But Ms. Duffy wasn't able to answer as one after another, colleagues came in and embraced her. "You astound me!" Mrs. Willoughby said, pressing her clasped hands to her lips, a gesture she normally bestowed upon seniors who were making their final appearance in the spring choral concert. Ms. Duffy looked easily as triumphant and beautiful as them. Her face shone; her long light hair flared out behind her; gone was the faint grimace that had once been her expression in repose. The change seemed complete and irreversible; this wasn't like the first week of school, when the teachers wore shorts and sundresses and still had their summer tans. Ms. Hempel remembered the shock of seeing Mr. Polidori's firm, hairy calves rising up from a pair of glistening orange sneakers— but within days, everyone looked haggard again and it was as if summer had never happened.

"Have you seen your kids?" asked Ms. Cruz, the assistant librarian. "They'll go crazy."

"They will freak!" Ms. Mulcahy said. "Suzanne, where's the sixth grade now? Are they at lunch?"

"Gym. That's all I've heard this year: Ms. Duffy, Ms. Duffy. They can't write their own names without mentioning Ms. Duffy."

"I missed them," said Ms. Duffy, vaguely.

"Maybe you'll want to wait until they've had a few minutes to cool off. You know how sweaty they can get playing basketball. And you won't believe how big they are. Huge. Amy Weyland is wearing a bra now."

From his cubicle, Mr. Meacham moaned, "Must we?"

And Mrs. Willoughby, peering into her coffee, said, "That girl's going to have a great little figure."

"Amy Weyland?" Ms. Duffy echoed.

"Yes! Can you believe it?" Ms. Olin, teacher of sixth-grade Humanities, nearly shouted. She appeared slightly feverish; in fact, everyone did, everyone seemed eager and a little overheated. There was so much to tell: Jonathan Hamish got suspended; Travis Bent went on medication; Mr. Peele agreed to turn on the air-conditioning early, even though it was only the beginning of May. And oh—the computer lab was finally done! Ms. Duffy needed to be apprised, and ushered back into the world they all had in common. The merry, frantic din of school rose up around them, louder and louder, as Yemen, fascinating and dusty, drifted farther away.

Ms. Hempel still held the photograph that she wanted to know more about. She would have her chance, eventually; she and Ms. Duffy were friends, school friends, in the sense that they had belonged to the same group of youngish teachers

who adjourned to a dark Irish bar as soon as the bell rang
on Friday afternoons. Returning the picture to its pile, she
gathered up her untouched books, wondered if her failure to
reread act 2 of *Romeo and Juliet* would prevent her from spark-
ing a spirited class discussion (maybe she'd just ask them to
act out their favorite scenes instead; the boys could cheerfully
spend an entire period bellowing, "Do you bite your thumb at
us, *sir?*"), and watched as Ms. Duffy was escorted out of the
faculty lounge, in search of her former fifth graders.

"Look who's here," cried Ms. Olin, leading the way.

The whole display was affecting but naive. Ms. Hempel
imagined a procession moving in stately fashion down the
middle school corridors, cheering administrators, a swaying
litter, children tossing flower petals and pencil shavings in
its path. Ms. Duffy was back! Once more there would be field
trips to Chinatown for soup dumplings, and scavenger hunts
in the botanical gardens, and sing-alongs to the Meat Puppets and other college-radio stars of the '80s. Once more the
Temple of Dendur would be erected in all its cardboard and
tempura glory. The final bittersweet pages of *Tuck Everlasting*
would again be read aloud in Ms. Duffy's husky, choked-up
voice. Fifth graders of the world, rejoice!

But Ms. Hempel knew better. Ms. Duffy was merely stopping by. She knew as soon as she saw her: Anna Duffy wasn't
ever coming back, even after her big hard belly resolved itself into a baby. Most likely necessity prompted this visit; she
probably needed to empty her locker, or roll over her retire-
ment plan. Didn't the others see? She was no longer one of
them; at some point during her year, she had turned away.
Slipped into her civilian clothes and disappeared. And if she
was back now, it was only to say good-bye or—if Ms. Hempel

were writing the script—So long, suckers! A farewell so improbable, it made Ms. Hempel laugh.

The Irish bar was only a few blocks away from their school. Beautiful Ms. Cruz, who really did lead the fabled double life of librarians, had discovered it one night while careening through town with a free jazz drummer nearly twice her age. Mooney's had been their last stop. What must Ms. Cruz have been thinking when she stepped out onto the sparkling, empty avenue, her head resting against the drummer's shoulder, dawn only an hour away, and saw that she was literally around the corner from her desk, her rubber stamps, her little stack of late notices? Maybe she was thinking, How perfect. To feel one's real life rub up so closely, so carelessly, to one's school life—there was no greater enchantment. Or so Ms. Hempel supposed, having never put enough distance between the two to experience it herself. She liked to hear Ms. Cruz talk, in her mild and self-effacing way, about all the old musicians she had fallen for. The hard-drinking drummer included. Ms. Cruz took him home with her that night, and then on Friday she took the teachers to Mooney's.

The narrow space was illuminated by strings of colored Christmas lights and a glowing clock. A jukebox stood in the back, in between the cavelike entrances to two bathrooms whose affiliation with any particular sex was never rigidly observed. Black battered tables, high unsteady stools, linoleum floor. The floor was wonderful to dance on. It made Ms. Hempel feel very graceful and coordinated, even before she started drinking. All the teachers loved to dance on Friday afternoons. They did the Hustle. They did the Electric Slide. The sticky blinds on Mooney's windows were always pulled shut, so it was easy to forget that it was only four o'clock and the sun was still shining outside and no one had come home from work yet. They danced as if it were the middle of the night. They did silly moves they remembered from high school and looked good doing them. When Mr. Radovich tried to dance like he was black, no one minded. They were too happy feeding quarters into the jukebox, shimmying to the bar and back. As she bumped hips with Ms. Cruz and sashayed toward the bathrooms, Ms. Hempel realized that she was actually meant to spend her whole life dancing, like those characters in the Ice Capades who go about their daily business on skates.

For someone who had an abundance of freckles and almost always wore clogs, Ms. Duffy could dance astonishingly well. She shook back her hair and half closed her eyes and lifted her chin ever so slightly, as if a handsome, invisible person were tilting up her face to kiss her. And then she stepped from side to side, with a barely discernible lilt in her hips, her spine long and straight, her shoulders faintly twitching, the movement small, purposeful, precise, and entirely effortless. It was the simplest dance in the world. And also the most beguiling, somehow. It inspired a feeling of great confidence in Ms. Duffy's body and the various things she could do with it. Other dancers drew close to her, unconsciously. She could often be found in the middle of a spontaneous dance sandwich. One afternoon Mr. Polidori sprang from his bar stool, cracked his knuckles, and then slid across the linoleum floor on his knees to arrive breathless at her neatly shuffling feet.

Ms. Hempel liked to think that this was the moment at which their grand passion began. Of course she could be wrong; Mr. Polidori performed sudden, extravagant gestures all the time—kissing your hand in gratitude, wrapping his fingers around your neck and gently throttling you, draping his arm across your shoulders with comradely indifference—gestures that thrilled Ms. Hempel whenever she happened, through luck and proximity, to be the recipient. Her skin on fire, she felt how ridiculous it was: Mr. Polidori, as a rule, could not be taken seriously. And Ms. Duffy did not appear to do so. After he came gliding across the floor, arms outspread, she merely offered him her hand and hoisted him up, never once losing the beat of her winsome little dance. But what if, as their hands joined, a secret message was exchanged? A message that took them both by surprise. Ms. Hempel wished that she had been sharp enough to catch the exchange; she thought of this moment only in retrospect, as she tried to make a story of what had happened. How interesting it would have been to witness the very inception of an affair! Or, rather, *a thing*; these days only married people were entitled to affairs. Either way, she could have hoarded up the image—he on his knees, she swaying above him—to share with Amit when he came home. Walking back dreamily from the bar, the afternoon light slanting across the pavement, Ms. Hempel was full of marvelous jokes and observations and stories to tell him. But then she went inside and it got dark; she turned up the television and felt a headache coming on, and by the time Amit returned from the lab, she couldn't think of anything to say, even when he wrinkled his nose and tranquilly asked, "How come you smell like cigarettes?"

Ms. Hempel wondered about the father of Ms. Duffy's baby. A sloe-eyed camel driver singing beneath his breath? A poet studying English at the university, or maybe a young doctor who led the way through a bazaar? She spent much of last period considering the possibilities. And if in her speculations she caught a whiff of something faintly rotten and imperial, she ignored it. Of all the wonderful novels E. M. Forster had ever written, *A Passage to India* was her favorite. It made her wonder, Were there any caves in Yemen? Caves that Ms. Duffy could have wandered in to explore, and then stumbled out, dazed and transformed.

At the entrance to the library, Ms. Cruz sat behind her enormous wraparound desk. It resembled a sort of cockpit, its high sides studded with librarian paraphernalia, Ms. Cruz wheeling expertly about the interior in her ergonomic chair. The desk had two levels; the lower level was intended for the librarian's use as she tried to do her work, while the higher level was meant for those standing around the desk and bothering the librarian. It was chest-high, the ideal spot for quickly finishing one's math problems before class, or asking importunate questions about the fate of the dinosaurs, or resting one's elbows, as Mrs. Willoughby was now doing, and speaking in confidential tones with Ms. Cruz below.

"Did you see—" Mrs. Willoughby turned to Ms. Hempel with excitement. Then she remembered. "Oh yes, you were there. Isn't she gorgeous?"

Ms. Hempel said, "Gorgeous. And very—" She extended her arms.

"I know, I know! Not what we expected. I thought she'd come back with a slide show and some nice scarves. But no! So much more."

She leaned toward Ms. Cruz, resuming: "Thirty-five miles from the nearest hospital. Is that madness?"

"There's a midwife. She'll be fine."

"Of course she will be. But still. Out in the middle of nowhere? With your first child? You have no idea."

"She was tired of living here. She said so all the time."

"You girls don't know what it's like. You get lonely at the beginning. You're tired, your nipples hurt, you can't remember what day it is."

"Roman will be there. And they're building a second yurt," Ms. Cruz said firmly, and then glanced up at Ms. Hempel. "Anna is moving upstate," she explained.

But that explained nothing. "A yurt?" Ms. Hempel asked. "Is that something . . . Yemenese?"

She blushed.

"Mongolian," Mrs. Willoughby said. "I had to ask, too. Don't worry; I won't tell Meacham. Not everybody who teaches here is a walking encyclopedia. It's a big circular tent made out of animal skins. Or, in Anna's case, some fancy, state-of-the-art, flame-retardant fabric." In the air, Mrs. Willoughby conjured up a miniature yurt with her hands. "Not like a teepee, more like a circus tent. Made out of yaks."

With a laugh and a wave, she demolished the little dwelling.

"But the father," asked Ms. Hempel, "is he from Yemen?"

Mrs. Willoughby looked at her peculiarly. "Heavens, no."

For the trip abroad had been cut short. Something in the food made Anna sick, dangerously so. Only two months out of the country and she was doubled over, shitting water. Thus the end of the lyrical e-mails. She had lost nearly twenty pounds by the time she crept onto the airplane and came home to convalesce at her mother's; it was there, looking pale and otherworldly, that she met Roman. A kite artist.

"He was visiting his mother, too," said Ms. Cruz.

"They're neighbors in the condo complex, the one her mother moved to after the divorce," said Mrs. Willoughby. "Anna claims that it's soulless and horrible. But maybe she feels differently now."

"Wow," said Ms. Hempel, collecting herself. So the father of Ms. Duffy's baby was an American, met early one morning in the courtyard of an ugly condominium.

"Being a kite artist—that's his job?" she heard herself asking.

Ms. Cruz nodded. "He's a master. You can find him on the Internet."

"He spends all day making kites?"

"And flying them."

"How wonderful," Ms. Hempel said uncertainly. "I'd like to do that."

"Oh, wouldn't we all?" Mrs. Willoughby said, and took a great breath, and for a precarious moment it looked as if she might sing the opening chorus of "Let's Go Fly a Kite." But then the opportunity softly passed. "There's family money, too, of course. And a big piece of land passed down through the ages. Anna is living on an estate! In a yurt, admittedly, but still. Pretty grand. Isn't this what they would call marrying up?"

"She got married?" Ms. Hempel asked, startled. She hadn't seen a ring.

A delicate look passed between the two other women. Ms. Hempel caught it, and felt herself go warm.

"It happened very quickly," said Ms. Cruz.

"As it so often does," added Mrs. Willoughby. "One minute you're all alone and the next—boom!—you're standing there in city hall with the man of your dreams."

"And moving upstate," Ms. Hempel said. "And having a baby."

"Exactly," Mrs. Willoughby said, with a slap of her hands on the top of Ms. Cruz's desk. "That's the trick of life, how much everything can change."

And then, squeezing Ms. Hempel's arm, she asked, "Remember? Anna was *miserable*."

BUT MS. HEMPEL WOULDN'T have described her as miserable nor, she doubted, would Ms. Duffy have ever used the word herself. Because didn't misery imply a wallowing sort of wretchedness? And a teacher had no time for that. The curriculum was always marching on, relentlessly: the scrambling dash from one unit to the next, the ancient Egyptians melting into the ancient Greeks, the blur of check marks and smiley faces, the hot rattling breath of the photocopier, book reports corrected shakily on the bus, the eternal night of parent-teacher conferences, dizzy countdowns to every holiday, and the dumb animal pleasure of rest. One could be quite unhappy and never have the chance to know it. Ms. Hempel was sometimes astonished by the thoughts she'd have while walking to work: one morning, she looked longingly at a patch of ice on the pavement and realized that if she were to fall and fracture her leg in several places, then she wouldn't have to go to school. And maybe, if the doctors put her in traction, a substitute would be hired for the rest of the year. Or maybe a body cast.

There was a way out, an honorable and dignified way out. All she had to do was undergo a terrible accident. . . .

But then her desk would be emptied, and every one of her secrets would come scuttling forth: the torn and smelly pair of stockings, abandoned there months ago, the descriptive paragraphs she took so long to grade that she finally claimed to have lost them at the laundromat, the open bag of Doritos. And, embarrassment aside, she had responsibilities: the volleyball finals were fast approaching—who would keep score? Someone else would have to chair the weekly meetings of the girls' after-school book group, and conduct the middle school assembly on Diversity Day. And who would finish grading the *Mockingbird* essays, adhering to the Byzantine rubric she'd devised?

The fact was, no one could.

"Call in sick," Amit would say sleepily, his arm flung over her. "Tell them you caught a cold." He'd kiss her. "You're infected. And extremely contagious. You need to stay in bed, okay?" But she would already be staggering toward the shower.

Did Ms. Duffy ever think about slipping on the ice? Probably not; her thoughts likely took a more enraged and sensible turn; probably, as she waited for the bus, she drafted letters of resignation in her head, letters that described in withering detail the incompetence of the new middle school director, or the shabby state of the women's bathroom on the second floor. Ms. Hempel suspected that such letters existed because Ms. Duffy was so thoroughly equipped when it came to complaining. They all loved to do it, of course, just as they all loved to dance, but she could outshine everyone. She would begin drily enough, with a sigh and a little self-mocking smile, but soon the full force of her indignation would take over, and her complaints would build in hilarity and ire until she was magnificent to behold—her whole self radiant with fury—so that Ms. Hempel shook her head and wondered how poor Mr. Mumford, even in his most ill-conceived moments of middle school leadership, could ever think it wise to say, "Now, Anna, just *calm down*." Often her stories ended with Mr. Mumford saying these words, or a variation thereof, and even when recollected in the yeasty tranquility of Mooney's, they still made Ms. Duffy utter a murderous, strangled scream.

"Aaaaaaaaarrrrrrrrr!"

From the end of the bar, Mr. Polidori would raise his glass to her.

The gesture was perfectly in character: joking, wry, yet also somehow gallant. He would then return his attention to Mimi Swartz, the person whose company he enjoyed more than anyone else's. She ran the art department, and made sculptures out of giant nails, was fifteen years his senior and went on long bike trips with her girlfriend. And he, as a teacher of physics, seemed always full of things to say to her. A mystery. But no more a mystery than his affair with Anna Duffy, who was once again complaining operatically.

AFFAIRS. FLINGS. APPARENTLY they happened all the time, and between the people you would least expect.

"You didn't know about me and Phil?" asked Ms. Cruz. Phil Macrae taught life science to the sixth grade. Beardless and cow-licked, he looked as if he had completed the sixth grade only recently himself. She had also had sex with Mr. Rahimi, the computer teacher, and Jim, who ran the after-school program.

"It got a little weird," she said.

Things also got weird for Mrs. Bell and Mr. Blanco; so weird, in fact, that he had to go teach at another school for a few years until the conflagration finally died out.

"Julia?" Ms. Hempel cried in dismay. She loved Julia Bell.

"This was ages ago. Long before you came to us," Mrs. Willoughby said.

"But Daniel?" Ms. Hempel cried. "I thought maybe he was gay."

"Oh no. No. Whatever gave you that idea? He's just Spanish."

And, incredibly, the former lover of Mrs. Bell. With his

pointed goatee and his funny little vests? It was very hard to picture. Perhaps, in a younger version, what Ms. Hempel found vague about his sexuality was actually dashing, irresistible. So much so that Julia Bell—a teacher blessed with pluck and humor and sense—risked everything to be with him.

"This was before the boys were born?" Ms. Hempel asked.

"Wally was two, I think, and not yet in school. But Nathan had already started kindergarten." Mrs. Willoughby raised her eyebrows. "It could have been a real mess."

Unthinkable, Julia making a mess. Which was exactly why Ms. Hempel adored her: the serene, amused, and capable air; the way she kept an easy sense of order among even the most fractious children; the affection that her sons heaped upon her, tackling her in the middle of the hallway. She also had a plume of pure white hair growing from her right temple, like Susan Sontag if she had gone into eighth-grade algebra. Her husband taught math, too, at the state university; they had fallen in love during graduate school. And all this—her world of boys and equations and good cheer—had been hazarded.

And then recovered.

Now she could sit in faculty meetings with Daniel Blanco and not show the slightest sign that he was in any way different to her from all the other staff members assembled around the room. If it weren't for the older teachers like Mrs. Willoughby, who remembered, there wouldn't be a trace left of that strange and perilous affair. Ms. Hempel couldn't decide which amazed her more: the sight of Mrs. Bell and Mr. Blanco talking amiably by the coffee urn, or the thought of them locked in an ancient, urgent, hopeless embrace.

———

LEAVING THE LIBRARY, Ms. Hempel was surprised to see Ms. Duffy standing alone in the vestibule, her hands resting lightly atop her belly. She seemed to have lost her entourage somewhere along the way. She was looking at the enormous bulletin boards that lined the walls and displayed the latest projects generated by the younger grades. Only a year ago she had been responsible for filling such a board, which required judiciousness (for not every child's hieroglyph could be hung) and a protracted wrestle with crepe paper and a staple gun. But now she was freed of that. What an escape! She gazed at the artwork with the cool eye of an outsider.

"Beatrice," Ms. Duffy said, and Ms. Hempel gave her a hug. The belly turned out to be as hard as it appeared.

"Have you seen this?" Ms. Duffy asked. She was studying one particular display. "They're overlapping. You can't read them. And he put a staple right through that kid's name."

He being Mr. Chapman, Wall Street trader turned teacher, called in to replace Ms. Duffy for the year, and now, it seemed, quite possibly for good.

"How are we supposed to know who drew the Minotaur?" She pointed at the bulletin board. "A child spent hours— hours!—working on this, and you can't even read her name."

"I hadn't noticed," Ms. Hempel said, peering. "But you're right. The name is kind of obscured."

"My god," Ms. Duffy muttered. "This isn't rocket science."

She reached up and pinched the staple between her thumb and forefinger. With a worrying motion of her hand she extracted it, and then flicked it to the ground like a cigarette butt.

"There," she said.

The child's name was Lucien Nguyen.

"Much better," Ms. Hempel said, and smiled. She wanted

to leave, her curiosity deadened; now that she knew Ms. Duffy wasn't harboring a little half-Yemenese baby, she no longer felt a strong need to talk with her. But she didn't like the way Ms. Duffy was still eyeing the display. And Ms. Hempel's tendency to suggest precisely the opposite of what she actually wished, in the vague and automatic hope of pleasing someone, asserted itself.

"Do you want to walk to Izzy's and get a bubble tea? My treat?"

For a moment it looked as if Ms. Duffy was about to agree. But just as she was turning away from the displays, she inhaled sharply and wheeled back around to stare at the bulletin board.

Her finger landed on a pink piece of paper and circled a single word with baleful vigor. "Did you see *this*?"

Ms. Hempel stepped closer to read the text, printed in a computer's version of girlish handwriting: *Persephone picked up the pomegranate and ate four of its' seeds.* She winced.

"Oooph. Not good."

Ms. Duffy held the word pinned beneath her finger. Or could it even be called a word? It didn't rightfully exist outside of the grammatical underworld, but Ms. Hempel knew from her own observations (in newspaper headlines! on twenty-foot billboards!) that these crimes were spreading. Rapidly. And evidently unchecked.

"They're kids," Ms. Duffy said. "They're learning, they make mistakes. But how are they going to know that they're mistakes if their teacher hangs them up on the fucking wall? I mean, does he make them do drafts? Does he *correct* anything?"

Ms. Hempel shrugged weakly. Her own alertness to error had wavered over the years. But maybe all it took was some time away, some time abroad, for one's acuity to be restored, because now, by simply standing beside Ms. Duffy, she could feel her powers beginning to return, she could see the mistakes leaping out at her, the bulletin board lighting up with offenses like the big maps she imagined they used at the FBI.

"Upper right-hand corner," she reported. "Completely random capitalization. Since when is *swan* a proper noun? Or *rape*, for that matter?"

Though she had to admit, both choices had their own logic.

She also spotted *Aries, alter* in the place of *altar*, and— there it was again—that old devil, *its'*. The real wonder of it all was how these mistakes managed to survive under the pitiless eye of spell-checking. You had to kind of love them for it, for enduring.

But Ms. Duffy felt no such affection. She was pulling Persephone right off the wall. "Where's Leda?" she demanded.

Ms. Hempel pointed reluctantly at the display. There was now a naked, pockmarked hole on the board. "Up there," she said, and stole a look down the hallway. Maybe Mr. Mumford or, even better, Mr. Peele would make a sudden and sobering appearance.

Ms. Duffy had risen up onto the very tips of her clogs, as if they were toe shoes and she a young dancer. Her belly didn't throw off her balance at all. Up, up, her puffy fingers reached, quivering with purpose. "Got it," she gasped. Down came Leda. Down, too, came Hera and the peacock, Echo and a weedy-looking Narcissus, Danaë dripping wet in her shower of gold. Down came the Minotaur and Medusa, Hermes, Neptune, Athena leaping bloodily from her father's splitting head. Neptune? Wasn't that the name the Romans used?

Exactly, said Ms. Duffy's scrabbling hands.

She thrust the rustling pile at Ms. Hempel. "Can you hold this for me?" she asked, out of breath, then rose up again on her toes.

Ms. Hempel gazed at the pillaged display, felt afraid, and looked frankly down the hallway, in the direction of help. But it didn't appear as if the authorities would be arriving anytime soon. She wondered briefly why she, of all the young teachers who drank too much at Mooney's, had been chosen by Ms. Duffy for this particular mission. Perhaps it was simply chance. The end of the day, an empty vestibule, a surge of nameless emotion—and then someone emerges, making you not alone anymore. So it had happened, a year ago, with Mr. Polidori. "Out of the blue?" Ms. Hempel had asked Ms. Duffy. "The two of you just—" She could not believe it then; she had wanted more—but now, holding the plundered goods against her chest, it made a sort of sense to her. It was possible to find oneself, without warning or prelude, *involved.* So she crouched down and tapped the papers against the floor, neatening the pile, making a crisp little sound, wanting above all to avoid the appearance of untowardness, wanting the whole operation to feel as tidy, as considered, as possible.

THEY AGREED, FINALLY, that the best thing to do would be to return the projects to Mr. Chapman's classroom, with a carefully worded note attached. *My room* was how Ms. Duffy referred to it, and then she alarmed Ms. Hempel by asking, "You're going to sign it, too?" No, she was not; but she didn't have the heart to say so yet, especially now that Ms. Duffy was being seized by some fresh distress. As the fluorescent lights flickered on in the classroom, she looked about her wildly. Things were not as she had left them.

There were still the purple beanbags in the reading corner, and the jade plants were thriving, having been faithfully watered by Ms. Cruz. The record player was still there, too, although buried under stacks of handouts, and the Calder mobile still dangled from the ceiling. But the Indonesian shadow puppets were gone, and so were the poems.

"He took down my poems?" Ms. Duffy's voice was small. She had gone to great lengths to procure them, risking arrest. A few years earlier, the poems began appearing on subways and buses, in the place where advertisements for credit repair and dermatologists had once hung. And as soon as a new poem was posted, Ms. Duffy would devise a plan for obtaining it: scouting out empty subway cars, climbing up onto the scarred seats, easing the poem from its curved plastic sheath, secreting it away beneath her long winter coat. All for the sake of her fifth graders! Every day they could gaze up and contemplate the words. Or not, and therein lay the beauty of osmosis. They passed the year in the company of Whitman and Dickinson, Mark Strand and May Swenson; some of it would penetrate even the most obdurate souls.

Which was probably the thinking of the transit authorities, as well; but the fact that her fifth grade's edification came at the expense of the citizenry's did not seem to give Ms. Duffy pause. And then it became possible to acquire the poems lawfully by sending off a simple request on school letterhead— but Ms. Duffy, like all true teachers, had a renegade spirit, and continued to haunt the buses late at night.

Now, in the place of her stolen poems were boldly colored posters urging the class to READ! Also pointing out that READING IS FUN! That people everywhere should CELEBRATE READING! Additionally, there was a poster commemorating the Super Bowl win of the Green Bay Packers. All of which, it was obvious, had been obtained through official channels.

Ms. Duffy sank down onto one of the many little tables arranged throughout the room. The fifth graders didn't yet know the isolation of desk-chairs; they still worked companionably at these low shiny tables. She covered her face with her hands and sighed, her elbows digging into the high mound of her stomach.

"I hope he put them somewhere safe," she said.

"You want me to send them to you?" Ms. Hempel asked.

"No, there's no room. I just meant in case he changes his mind."

She glanced over at what had once been her desk, at the piles she was no longer accountable for.

"He has them doing those dumb workbooks?" she asked, but all of her fire from the vestibule was now extinguished.

"It's his first year," Ms. Hempel said, and laid the ransacked myths on Mr. Chapman's desk. "He should take whatever shortcuts he can find."

Ms. Duffy didn't answer. She was still looking around the classroom, at the small ways it was now strange, at the names taped onto the backs of the chairs, names that had no meaning to her.

She said, "I lost Theo McKibben at the Metropolitan Museum. My first year."

"Theo?" Ms. Hempel laughed. "That's easy to do."

"It was a nightmare. My first waking nightmare."

"The first of many," said Ms. Hempel. "But just think: You'll never have to go on a field trip again."

Ms. Duffy smiled slightly. "Never again."

And then Ms. Hempel realized with a sickened feeling

that she had forgotten to distribute the permission slips for next week's outing to the planetarium. Only three days left: not a problem for the organized ones, but it didn't allow much leeway with the children you always had to hound for everything. She would have to resort to an incentive plan: Early dismissal? Ice cream?

She paced around the desk mindlessly and saw it as both hopeful and doomed: the careful stacks beginning to slip, colored pens littered everywhere, memos from Mr. Mumford protruding at odd angles, the plastic in-box taken over by trading cards, half-eaten candy bars, extra-credit assignments on the verge of being lost.

"You're brilliant." She turned to Ms. Duffy. "You are. Because we can't leave to make more money; that's despicable. And we can't leave to do something easier, some nice quiet job in an office; that would be so embarrassing! Am I supposed to tell my kids, 'Okay, I'm off to answer phones at an insurance company'? It's impossible. So what can we do? We can always . . ." Ms. Hempel gestured helplessly at Ms. Duffy's belly. "Why didn't I think of that?"

She had imagined a body cast instead.

Again Ms. Duffy gave a thin smile. It wasn't clear whether she took Ms. Hempel's compliment as such.

"So what's stopping you?" she asked idly. She plucked a long, loose hair from the sleeve of her sweater and dropped it onto Mr. Chapman's floor. Then suddenly she seemed to remember that she was herself pregnant, and undergoing a remarkable experience. She lit up. "You should do it!" she said with abrupt conviction. "You'll love it. You will." She stood from the little table and moved warmly toward Ms. Hempel. "We think we have all the time in the world, but in reality we don't. And when you find the right person, you just have to go for it. There's never a good time; it's never convenient; don't fool yourself into waiting for the perfect time—"

She stopped. Her hands flew up to her mouth. "I'm so sorry!"

Ms. Hempel touched the fair, freckled arm. "Oh, don't worry. Please, really, don't worry."

"I'm an idiot," cried Ms. Duffy.

"You're not," said Ms. Hempel. "Because I forget, too. After I do the dishes, I get this panicked feeling that I've put my ring down somewhere and now I can't find it." She picked up her bare hand and looked at it. "Everything was friendly, it really was."

Ms. Duffy nodded, her face stricken.

"Amit and I still talk on the phone. And last week he sent me a book." She didn't mention that it was actually one of her books, a book that had been swept up in his wake and had now washed up again on the shores of his new apartment. "We're in very good touch," she said.

Ms. Duffy remained unconsoled. "What happened?" she murmured. "What made you decide—"

It was hard to keep straight; they had told people different things at different times. There was Amit's fellowship in Texas, which he couldn't turn down; and there was the difficulty of finding time to plan a wedding, not to mention the expense; there was their youth, of course, and the uncertainty that comes with it, the fearful cloudiness of the future (and what a mercy that was, to be considered, at nearly thirty, still heartbreakingly young). . . . All of which was true of course, just as all of it was prevarication, and even in the midst of saying these things, she was never sure exactly whose feelings were being spared, just who was being protected. For whose sake was all this delicacy required? She hated to think that it might be hers.

"It wasn't the teaching, was it?" asked Ms. Duffy.

Oh no, it wasn't that. At least she didn't think so. But funny how everyone had a theory they believed yet also wished to see refuted. "It's not your father, is it?" her mother asked, her father dead two years now but his absence still brimming as his presence once had. When she showed her the ring, her mother had offered to walk her down the aisle. "But I know it's not the same," she said. "I know that."

So she had told her mother no, it wasn't because she missed her father. Though she still could feel his warm, dry, insistent hand hovering just above the top of her head. And she had told Mr. Polidori no, it wasn't because of him, either. Though at moments she could still feel his hand, too, as it made its way down the length of her spine. She had been surprised that he'd even asked. A surprising glimpse of vanity, of self-importance. He had cornered her by the jukebox and gazed down at her earnestly—the earnestness also a surprise.

But it was only a kiss!

And some nuzzling, some breathless pressing and hugging, in one of Mooney's indeterminate bathrooms. Ages ago, on one of those happy Friday afternoons. After he had ended things with Ms. Duffy but before he had fallen for the gamine younger half sister of Mimi Swartz. A pause between the acts, there in the dark stall at Mooney's, everyone giddy with the fast approach of summer. She had tumbled into the bathroom and found him, back to the door, penis presumably in hand, and before she could even gasp he had glanced over his shoulder, told her to wait, and then unhurriedly finished, washed his hands, dried them from a roll of gray paper towels, asking her, Do you hate this song as much as I do? They had danced, barely able to move. He had lowered the swinging latch into the little round hook by the door.

Forgot to do that, he said, and she laughed.

Or did she? She would like to think that she had, that she had kept her wits about her and laughed, kept things floating along lightly, the encounter accidental and jolly. She would like to think that she hadn't swooned. Hadn't shut her eyes and given way, tipped her head and held on. There was no hesitation—only treachery, only readiness—a perfect swan dive into the dark pool of flings and affairs. Maybe she had let out a little moan. But then the song came to an end, and he clasped her bearishly, pecked her on the forehead, said: I bet you make all the boys crazy, Ms. Hempel. And after releasing the latch, gallantly held the door open for her.

She walked, obedient, to her seat at the bar, wondering, What just happened?

Later, she would return to this moment, flipping it back and forth like a tricky flash card, one that somehow refused to be memorized. She asked herself all the boring questions (not pretty enough? odd smell? fiancé?) but couldn't quite manage an answer. Causality kept escaping her. He kissed her, then he changed his mind—that was as far as she ever got. But always fascinating to her was fact that she could *feel* him changing his mind. Feel it in her muscles and on her skin. Not that he did anything so obvious as stiffen, and his body didn't once let go of hers; yet something shifted: the pressure that was once excited now merely emphatic, the mouth still warm but only reassuringly so, the embrace turning into a squeeze. His body's gracious withdrawal of interest in the very moment that he decided, No, this really isn't for me.

And though many things would reveal themselves in

time—the sex of Ms. Duffy's baby, a girl; and the name, Pina, after the bleak choreographer; the name of the woman who worked at Amit's lab, which was Lilly; the right word, the word she'd been looking for, *Yemeni*—still she returned to the bathroom at Mooney's, to its perfect mystery, to the moment when Mr. Polidori wrapped his arms around her like a bear. So that was what it felt like, someone making a decision. She wanted to remember how it felt.

Satellite

Ms. HEMPEL HAD A WAY with girls of a certain age. They hung around her after school; they invited her over to their houses for dinner. They sent notes at the end of the year, usually on cards they had drawn themselves. Serpentine flowers. Primitive stars. On overnight trips they asked if they could play with her hair. They showed her their poems, sought advice about boys. At Christmas they gave her poinsettias and a gift certificate for a back massage. They liked her shoes, her clothes; they liked every time she did something different with her hair. Not once did they miss her birthday. On the last day of school, they hugged her, speechlessly. But later she would read, in their purple handwriting: *I'll always remember the seventh grade.*

Her sister, Maggie, found all of this difficult to believe. "I would never do that for a teacher," she declared. "Is your school a hippie school?" She wanted to know if they had to do gym. "Can they call you Beatrice?" She narrowed her eyes. "Do they get real grades?"

"Of course they do!" Beatrice said, and snatched the birthday card back from her sister. "I *failed* a kid two years ago."

Maggie returned to her puzzle book, spread out on the kitchen table. She resumed chewing the beleaguered eraser at the end of her pencil. Rotating her ankle, she kneaded her long monkey toes against the floor.

"I don't know," she said. "Your students sound weird."

According to whom! But Beatrice contained herself. She gazed at her sister—the shiny, pebbled dome of her forehead, the butterfly appliqués on her mall-bought top, the chapped knuckles of her long, desiccated fingers—and thought to herself, without much pleasure, My students would eat you for breakfast.

Did Maggie even know what it meant to shape an eyebrow? To do an ollie? Would she say tuna sashimi was her favorite food ever? Would she choose Elie Wiesel as the subject for her next book report?

Probably not. She wasn't in any hurry to become a knowing, complicated member of the world. She was content to do puzzles and enter flute competitions and behave ingratiatingly with their mother. Often Beatrice had to remind herself that her sister was the same age as the girls she taught at school. Compared to them, Maggie seemed either stunted or strangely wizened.

"No tea for me," she said, though Beatrice hadn't asked. She poured the boiling water into a cup and opened the refrigerator.

"Where's the milk?"

"You'll have to use soy," Maggie said. "Turns out I'm lactose intolerant."

"But we love milk," said Beatrice. "We love all dairy products."

"Remember last summer? The banana split?"

Beatrice nodded, haunted not by the explosive sounds emanating from the bathroom but by the hoarse moans coming from what must have been her sister. She had sounded like an old sinner on his deathbed.

"Well, that was the problem," Maggie said.

Beatrice shook the little box of liquid soy. She shook and shook, but didn't have any plans to open it. "Mama puts this in her coffee?"

"Mama didn't even drink her first glass of milk," Maggie crowed, "until she was seven years old!" No wonder she looked so pleased with her deficiency. Once upon a time, there was no such thing as milk in China! She could have stepped right out of the mythical rice fields herself. Not like Beatrice, or their brother Calvin: those shaggy, beetle-browed, milk-drinking mutts. Maggie's hair was straight and black, her limbs as dreamily smooth as their mother's—as if she had managed to run the gestational gauntlet unscathed by their father's messy genes. That mysterious soup, full of slashes: German/Scottish/Welsh/Irish/French. Really, French? Or was that just a wishful affectation? No one knew anymore, no one cared; so why not be a tiny bit French and marvel at Maggie's quality of chinoiserie. She was not quite the real deal, although she looked pretty close. So much like her mother, people said of Maggie, a similarity that Beatrice had never been accused of.

"Did Mama tell you?" Maggie said. "You're supposed to be helping me with my application essay."

"It's my birthday!" Beatrice said.

She was supposed to be eating noodles for longevity and then maybe some cake for sheer sugary happiness. (But cake with a tall, cold glass of soy?) She was supposed to be blowing out candles and making wishes and being waited upon by her mother. Sleeping late in her narrow bed, reading her old Madeleine L'Engle books, flipping through her record collection in the closet. Why not come home? Her mother's invitation on the phone had been seductive. Why not come home and relax?

"I don't know my teachers' birthdays," Maggie said musingly. "So I couldn't give them a card even if I wanted to." She looked with new curiosity at Beatrice. "How do your students know when your birthday is?"

Beatrice lifted her hands in self-defense. "It comes up naturally in conversation!" she cried.

MAGGIE HAD BEEN, FROM the very first, a surprise. When they found out her mother was pregnant, Beatrice's father had already taken up residence in a clammy carriage house a few blocks away, basically living in someone else's backyard. It was only a trial separation, he said. He took with him six shirts, his English shaving kit, and a book of tormented divorce poems by Derek Walcott. Beatrice and Calvin would visit him on the weekends, playing cards on the Murphy bed while he cooked them cheese sandwiches in a toaster oven. Then their mother changed her mind, and he moved back home. With miraculous speed he finished building the gazebo that had been languishing for months. They switched therapists; they spent a weekend at an outdoor early-music festival; he bought her some extravagant chandelier earrings, and when she told him she didn't like them, he failed to act insulted. A delicate truce was established, into which Maggie was born.

"She's the caboose!" people said, which seemed a very lighthearted way of referring to an accident of such human proportions. At the time Beatrice couldn't bear to contemplate how such an accident might have occurred. Only many years later did she realize that her sister sprang from a final good-bye—the product of one last, sad, habitual bout of affection—an insight that occurred while she herself was thus occupied, though in her case she remembered to wear a diaphragm.

Maggie's birth coincided with the release of a new Sonic Youth record called *Sister*. Beatrice went to the all-ages show they played on a Sunday afternoon and bought a T-shirt with a picture of a half-naked punk rock girl crawling along the floor and staring alluringly, or maybe crazily, at the camera. She was naked from the waist down, not on top. It was hard to tell, but it looked like she had carved some words into her leg with a razor or a pocketknife. Beatrice knew from reading the back of the album that this picture was a film still, and that the film was called *Submit to Me*, but she couldn't find the information she wanted most, which was where one could see a film like this.

At home she pointed to her chest, saying, "Look!" The shirt said SISTER, and was a tribute to the baby. Maybe because the silk screen wasn't very clear, no one seemed to notice that the crawling girl didn't have on any underwear, and Beatrice was able to sport her shirt everywhere, even to school. She wore it until it became as thin and soft as a little kid's nightgown. Then she kept on wearing it until a hole opened up beneath the armpit and another one at the neckline, and then until it completely fell apart. Thinking ahead, she kept the remains; she had a feeling they'd be of historical interest and value, and maybe, like a Civil War uniform, good material for a quilt.

"THERE IS NO GREATER JOY than seeing the fruit of your labor shining on the stage." So read the final sentence of Maggie's essay, a sentence that Beatrice feared would not immediately identify her sister as a gifted or talented youth. Maggie was applying to a special summer program, and she needed to get

in. Once she finished the eighth grade, she wouldn't be ushered onto the ancient, rolling campus where Beatrice and Calvin had spent their adolescence. She'd be going to a real high
school instead, with tracked classes and a chain-link fence.
Hence the grim work of supplementing her soon-to-be-public
education had begun.

"Okay, let's take a step back," said Beatrice. "What are you
trying to say in this essay? What do you want to communicate to the reader?"

"That I like being a theater tech," said Maggie.

"Okay, good. So what about it do you like?"

"I like getting to use the electric drill. Also, Mr. Minkoff
showed me how to work the circuit breaker." She thought
for a moment. "We can go to the cast party afterwards if we
want."

"Great. Those are really great specifics. Write those down."
Beatrice felt clearheaded, competent. Nearly professional. But
she couldn't get over the feeling that she was performing for
a tiny hidden camera feeding directly into her mother's busy
control room. "Now let's think a little broader. Be a little more
abstract. What are the *big* reasons you're drawn to doing this?
What do you get out of the experience?"

"Like, emotionally?" Maggie asked, full of sincerity, far
more tractable as a pupil than she ever was as a sibling. "I get
good self-esteem. Is that what you mean? And cooperation
and problem solving and self-respect." Looking at her final
sentence, she added neatly: "Joy. A lot of joy."

Beatrice took a breath. "All of those reasons are certainly
broad." She glanced down at the notebook page on which
her sister was steadfastly transcribing her ideas. The clichés,
nothing if not resilient, were massing once again; perhaps

a more drastic approach was required. "Now let's try going deeper, too. Let's try finding some darkness, some interesting conflict."

"Conflict like how?" Maggie asked. "You mean fights backstage?"

"Well, that's one sort, but I was thinking of the more internal kind."

Beatrice deliberated, but only briefly, then raised an unseen hand and placed it over the tiny hidden camera.

"And by internal, I mean the conflict you feel as a theater tech. The inner conflict. Doing all that hard work, but never really getting recognized. Not getting the appreciation you deserve. Having to stay in the wings the whole time."

Maggie had stopped writing, but she was still gazing at the half-filled page, as if she had found a menacing pattern there.

Beatrice's voice rose slightly. "Who spends all those hours painting and hammering and sawing? You do! But do you get to come out and take a bow? Do you get the applause?"

Maggie looked up. "At the curtain call, the actors point to us and we stick out our heads and wave."

The uncombed heads popping out, and the shy, puckish, manic waving—Beatrice could see it perfectly.

"That's nice," she said. "That really is. Those moments of recognition can feel wonderful." And she meant it, too—she did—but how could she help but also mention the injustice, the indignity, of being always the stagehand but never the star, always on tiptoe, the gentle mover and fixer, condemned to forever facilitate the dazzling achievements of someone else? Not too different, she saw, from her own line of work. On some days, at least. So she should know! "It just sounds hard to me," said Beatrice.

Maggie tapped her pencil against the kitchen table rapidly. It was clear that something had begun to stir and glow inside her, as hoped. The slow bubbling of ambivalence? The surfacing of secret trouble? Maggie finally held her pencil still. Without looking from her notebook, she said, "So you want me to write that I *don't like* being a theater tech?"

Surprised, Beatrice realized it was merely resentment she'd seen stirring, with herself as its object.

"Oh, Maggie, that's not what I mean. I'm not trying to put words in your mouth. I don't want to take something you love and turn it into something horrible. I just wanted to help you explore the ways in which this experience might be *complicated*."

"Not everything is complicated."

"But it is! It is!" cried Beatrice. "At least it is in writing. In good, interesting writing. Which is exactly what you're capable of, and what they'll be looking for in your essay."

She thought with despair of the small masterpiece that Emily Radinsky had turned in as her last book report, a sixteen-page first-person narrative imagined from the perspective of a minor character in Elie Wiesel's *Night*. It was so beautifully written, so profound in its understanding of family and loss, so simply and astonishingly great, that Beatrice had wept when she read it. She could almost weep now, just thinking of it, and looking at her earnest, resentful, circuit-breaking sister, and knowing how the good people in charge of enrichment programs everywhere would be banging down Emily's door, and not hers.

"Okay," said Beatrice, brightly. "Forget complicated. Let's try thinking about this from a different angle."

With a soft rustle of paper, Maggie turned to a new page.

———

As a very young child, she had been a biter. This was a source of consternation to her mother, developmental interest to her father, and to Beatrice, bottomless delight, serving as it did as proof of the baby's badass nature, and augury of transgressive acts to come. She liked to think that Maggie's early exposure to excellent and angry music had possibly played a role. Not just in terms of the biting itself but also, gratifyingly, in the general lack of remorse. "I bite Eli," Maggie would announce upon arriving home from the playground. "I bite Josh. I bite Georgie. I bite Priya." Sometimes she'd try to bite Beatrice, too, her chin jutting forward and a wild look coming into her eyes, but this did not in any way diminish Beatrice's enthusiasm. She just learned to move quickly out of reach; the attacks were swift and for the most part unpredictable. "I bite Mama," Maggie would say. "I bite Calvin." Looking on mildly from the sofa, their father said, "The real question is, what is she trying to tell us?"

Maybe she was trying to say, My teeth hurt. My T-shirt is scratchy. I don't want to wait my turn for the slide. I'm sick of the park, of the trees, of the picnic benches. I'm tired of sunshine and shade, of pita bread in plastic bags. I'm sick of my car, my yard, my crib, my house, and the friendly, baffled people who live there. The strange smell embedded in the carpet. The long dark painting above the fireplace. The breathless feeling in the air, as if everyone were about to turn around and disappear. All of them: the boy peering at his turtle in the tank, the girl clattering down the stairs and singing at the top of her lungs, the man hovering in the doorway, finger tucked in a half-closed book, and the woman making fireworks explode in the huge battered woks that teeter on the stove. Noisy, large, and omnipresent—so why does it feel as if one day they might all disappear?

Maggie clamped down on her father's salty forearm. Beatrice laughed. Calvin grimaced. Mama said something reproving. It was directed at Beatrice, not the biter. "Why did you bite Papa?" asked their father, looking into the eyes of the little girl. "Can you use your words and tell Papa?" Maggie pulled away and careened across the room with perfect indifference as Beatrice watched dumbly in wonder and envy. She had been plotting her own minor rebellions for years and had yet to cultivate this cavalier air. She would never be truly punk rock. She worried too much about making other people cross with her. Her hair was a police-light blue, her ears sparkling with hardware, her boots heavy enough to stomp someone senseless, and she still couldn't bring herself to spit out her gum on the sidewalk. *Nobody likes a litterbug,* she heard a voice saying. *Fuck you!* she told the voice, who simply chuckled. And now her mother was mad at her. Unbearable. Her black-haired, smooth-limbed, no-nonsense mother. What had she said? "You're making this harder." Or maybe, "You're not helping." Not cruel or cutting words, exactly, but enough to make you wither inside, especially when spoken by the person who was cooking you dinner, as she had every night for the past how ever many years, her silky arms scarred from the sputtering oil, scars that on anyone else would be mistaken for freckles.

But if given a choice, Beatrice would take disapproval—which was at least familiar, brisk, and suitably maternal—over the weird stare with which her mother now regarded her when she got home from school. As if Beatrice wasn't even her child anymore. Her mother would get this look in her eye—this stunned look—and she would gaze up at Beatrice hopefully, like she wasn't Beatrice at all but a neighbor's nice kid, a teenage babysitter come to the rescue. As if her very arrival meant that her mother could pick up her purse, point to the emergency list on the fridge, put on some lipstick, and walk out the door. Don't worry; the baby's sleeping. Calling over her shoulder. Beatrice dreaded this look. It made her feel queasy. It made her want to do the stupidest, most hopelessly un–punk rock thing—which was to screw up her face and cry, *Mama COME BACK.*

Their mother was outside in the cold, calling their names. She needed help. Beatrice looked out the kitchen window and saw her in the middle of the frozen yard, deep in contemplation of the gazebo. What was she holding? Was that really a hatchet? In the distance, the door to the toolshed gaped open. Maggie was already flying out the back door, red parka flapping. Their mother stalked around the little structure, her gardening clogs bright against the gray turf, her small black head covered entirely by the crocheted cloche hat that Maggie had produced in a fit of craftiness. Beatrice owned one, too, but didn't remember where she had put it. Slowly she followed her sister outside, wanting no part in any of this.

One hand occupied with the hatchet, Mama was using the other to grasp the yew bushes by the neck and shake them in an uncharitable way. They grew shaggily at the foot of the gazebo, loyal but disheveled sentries, planted there years before. It seemed that Mama had decided now was the moment to relieve them of their duties. When Beatrice, shivering in her swingy little car coat, suggested that the spring might be a better time, her mother said, "Who knows when you'll be coming home next?" and with a heavy feeling Beatrice realized that a definite and as yet undisclosed list, including such items as essay revision and tree removal, had been compiled in preparation for her visit.

"Don't you have anything more practical to wear?" her mother asked, looking askance at the car coat, and the only thing Beatrice could think to say was, "I've always liked those bushes. They just need to be pruned."

"They're hideous!" Maggie said, and for emphasis kicked at some lower branches with her sneaker. "We're going to plant wisteria instead. The vines will climb up over the roof and look romantic."

"It's a business decision. The bushes have a lot of spiders in them. They make the whole place feel dark." Mama lightly tested the blade of the hatchet with her fingertip. "No one's going to want to eat breakfast sitting next to those bushes."

Beatrice didn't know what her mother was talking about. She felt both outwitted and outnumbered, but wasn't ready yet to admit her disadvantage. Meanwhile, Maggie hopped about on the hard ground, waving her arms in the air as she draped the gazebo with prospective vines. "Maybe, if they're really beautiful, we can increase our rates."

She jigged some more, her fingers twitching in the happy act of counting money. She glanced coyly at Beatrice. "Maybe we'll even charge *you* for a visit."

"Don't be ridiculous," said their mother. It was unclear whether she meant the rate hike or the new policy regarding family members. In possible consolation she told Beatrice, "I'm going to find you some good work gloves," and headed off in the direction of the toolshed.

"Charge me?" Beatrice looked at her sister.

"I'm only teeeeeeasing!" Maggie shrieked, and jigged even faster, full of plans. Little seashell soaps! Little tiny bottles of shampoo! And extra towels, folded at the foot of the bed. Foil-wrapped chocolates to be placed on the pillows. Didn't that sound cozy? She swung gleefully around a gazebo post. There'd be discounts for repeat guests. An added charge during graduation week. But you also had to factor in the 10 percent finder's fee that went automatically to the agency. . . .

Beatrice tried to focus. She asked, "Are you talking about an *inn*?"

"A bed-and-breakfast!" corrected Maggie. She then added soberly, "To open an inn, we'd need to get a special license, and those cost a lot of money."

"We?"

"Me and Mama. We're business partners. Fifty-fifty."

"Good grief," said Beatrice, and wondered how long the two of them had been in cahoots. Probably forever. She imagined coming home again and finding them doing tai chi in their matching pajamas. A terrible joke. And which was more distressing—their merry collusion or the thought of strange people traipsing about her house, putting their feet up on the furniture? She felt, for a moment, an instinctive Victorian horror of one's family being in trade. She feared that the particular trade of hospitality would sink one even farther. Maybe they should just take in sewing, she thought miserably, picturing her sister's long, chapped, but clever fingers flying above a seam. But how could she harbor such detestable ideas? When had she become such a nervous little snob? She had aspired to anarchism once, or at least to a Billy Bragg sort of socialism. She'd made a romance out of what she called "regular people" who were experts at living what she called "normal life." Pickup trucks, domestic beer—delicious! At those punk rock shows on Sunday afternoons, she would lie about where she went to school, ashamed of the grassy quads and classes in French cinema. When asked, she would most often name the very school where Maggie, soon enough, would be walking through the battle-scarred doors. At a certain age, Beatrice had longed to go there herself.

"Look what I found!" their mother called, coming toward them and waving a handsaw. She looked pretty and rosy from the cold and Beatrice felt her heart lurch painfully.

"Are you planning to use my room?" she found herself asking, to her own dismay. This was not at all what she had wanted to say, especially in a voice that sounded high-pitched and sulky. "Using it as part of your business?"

Her mother frowned. "Beatrice, sweetheart. That room is always yours to stay in, whenever you want. You know that." She held out a pair of crusty gardening gloves.

"Are strangers going to be sleeping there?" The sulky voice persisted. "Don't you think that's risky, considering all the valuable things around?"

An opening: her mother nimbly leaped. All those old magazines, she said—they were a serious fire hazard. All those little knickknacks and photos gathering dust on the bookshelves. And what was Beatrice still keeping in her drawers? Certainly nothing she'd ever think of wearing again. In fact, her mother had picked up some empty cartons at the liquor store, and was hoping that over the weekend they could make a trip to the drop-off bin outside the church.

A little box floated beside another item on the list, waiting to be firmly checked.

"That's archival material, Mama!" The fanzines, the flyers, the packet of ketchup given to her by the drummer from the Volcano Suns. Her first leather jacket. Her first plaid schoolgirl skirt, pleated and saucy. Her first piece of black velvet, held together by safety pins. "You expect me to give away my *Sister* shirt?"

"You have an apartment," Maggie said. "You could keep it there."

"My apartment is minuscule!" Beatrice wailed. "We're talking about important cultural history here!"

Their mother laughed. "What do you want me to do? Keep your bedroom hermetically sealed? A shrine to your youth?"

"Well, yes." This was exactly what Beatrice wanted. A shrine. Dim, magical, hushed, undisturbed. Ideally climate controlled, so the vinyl wouldn't warp. She had never put it into words before, but this was precisely what she was looking for when she came back to the house where she grew up. And, as always, her mother had managed to divine her heart's desire. She had an uncanny ability to do so, which made her refusal to grant its secret wishes that much more exasperating. How had she known, one summer morning long ago, that Beatrice walked out the back door so purely delighted with herself, feeling like anything at all might occur that day, dressed as she was in torn T-shirt, leopard mini, ripped fishnets, red heels—an outfit ingeniously designed to disguise sluttiness as irony (So *Sid and Nancy!* she'd thought in the closet)—how had she known her daughter's happiness? And happened to drive from the post office to the market along the same route that Beatrice was tottering her way to the bus stop? Beatrice heard a car honking from behind (in appreciation, she'd thought) and was discouraged to turn around and find her heat-seeking mother, face aglow, hands wrapped tightly around the steering wheel. Somehow the episode—of thwarted desire; of surprise and humiliation—was remembered as a little piece of family comedy: an opportunity for Mama to roll her eyes and everyone to laugh about the time Bea left the house looking like an insane prostitute. And Beatrice knew even as she now spoke, even as she sighed, "Yes, actually, that's what I want," this very moment was becoming laughable, toothless, the time Beatrice tried to turn her bedroom into a museum.

"It's not like you're dead!" said Maggie cheerfully, and began kicking at the yew bushes again.

BUT THEIR FATHER WAS DEAD. It was impossible to come home and not think this thought every hour you were there. Maggie the biter had been right all along—everybody in that rackety house would disappear. First Beatrice, off grudgingly to college. Then Calvin, a few years later, with his towering backpack and his untouched passport. Their father next, falling to his knees on a tennis court. And their mother—still strictly present, of course, still standing there agitating her pans on the stove, but you could argue that she had been the first of them to leave. Beatrice wasn't sure, but she thought it might have happened when Papa moved into the carriage house. Something shifted then; some agreement was reached between their mother and solitude. "You have to understand, Chinese don't *get* divorced," she had said one night when Beatrice and Calvin returned from a long afternoon of cheese sandwiches and Hearts. But she said it with defiance. She said it with a strange sort of exultation. She would be doing what no one else in her family or her acquaintance had ever done. She'd go back to graduate school—something useful, like accounting? University administration? She'd make appearances at parties alone. She'd practice a wartime frugality, keeping wings of the big house unheated and the children in hand-me-down clothes. It was doable. It was demanded of her. She'd pull through; she'd find ways; she would manage. The thought terrifying, but also bracing—like jumping out onto an unknown highway from a car crowded with quarrelsome people and half-eaten bags of cheese doodles and loud staticky music on the radio. The car would screech off into the distance and she would be left by herself on the side of the road, putting one foot deliberately in front of the other, the wind whistling all around.

She would show them!

And so she would have, if not for that stubborn zygote. Who knew that at this late stage things could still take root? She had always given money to Planned Parenthood; she had no qualms in that regard, no qualms at all. Then why she did let nature follow its unruly course? It was the mystery lying at the deep heart of her. Or maybe the answer was simple: maybe she had for once in her life succumbed to sentiment, an occurrence so rare that it tended to confound her, like when she had paid to have Calvin's first sneakers preserved in bronze.

Unborn Maggie brought everyone home. The shaving kit took up its post in the bathroom; the book of poems returned to the shelf. But pointedly life did not resume where it had left off—upon his return, it was difficult to escape the feeling that their father was anything more than a longtime visitor, there on sufferance. His stay in the carriage house had made him older, and now, like an abashed and absentminded relative, he tried to keep out of their mother's way. Beatrice wondered if one day she and Calvin would sit down with Maggie over little glasses of sherry and, in the wistful manner of Russian émigrés, attempt to explain what life was like before. The fireflies, the linden trees, the dusky walk down to the edge of the lake—oh, such beautiful brawls! Their handsome father screaming and their lovely, long-haired mother in tears. (Someone forgot to pack the bathing suits.) Then the ceaseless, silent car rides home, with the rising moon close on their tail. The children carried up the staircase: girl in father's furry clasp, boy in mother's smooth one. Lying stiffly in bed, under the cool sheets, listening to more shouting from below. Or maybe instead (it was equally possible) to the sounds of the newspaper crackling, of something read aloud in a resonant voice, followed by elliptical laughter.

"And don't you remember?" Beatrice would ask eagerly of her brother. "Don't you remember the time we were all watching that dumb vampire movie—you know, the one with George Hamilton? We were watching it on Channel 56 and Papa comes into the room with his big Dracula laugh and your plastic fangs and a big glass of cranberry juice? He chased Mama all over the house . . ."

Incredible. Maggie would listen to their stories in disbelief. Are you talking about *my* father? *My* mother? She had grown up under an entirely different regime.

BACK INSIDE THEY EXAMINED their scratches, small and large. Everyone smelled agreeably piney. "Mission accomplished," said Beatrice darkly. She would have to take her car coat to the cleaners. Dazed, she and Maggie held their hands beneath the kitchen tap, warming their fingers in the stream of hot water, until their mother walked by and turned it off. She was moving about the room in her old ballet, reaching and dipping, opening and shutting, and Beatrice felt with relief that perhaps the weekend had finally begun: for here was her mother, making them something to eat.

Maggie stationed herself at the table and flipped open a puzzle book. Her mouth found the comforting eraser again. Beatrice watched as a heavy, blank calm settled over her sister's face.

"Hey!" said Beatrice. "Maggie! I have an idea. Why don't you read Mama your new essay?"

"She doesn't like being read to," said Maggie slowly. "She likes reading things for herself."

"She's right," said their mother, without turning from the counter.

At the far end of the table, Beatrice regrouped. "Not for her sake, for yours. Hasn't anyone told you about the benefits of reading your work aloud? I make all of my students do it. You pick up mistakes. You hear the rhythm of your sentences. It's a vital part of the revision process."

"Oh, all right." Maggie bent down wearily and dragged forth her backpack. Beatrice smoothed the tablecloth in front of her and tried to arrange her face into a disinterested expression. "Stand up," she instructed. "Use your diaphragm, it's good practice."

"Practice for what?" Maggie asked, but then did as she was told. She held herself erect and read clearly from her notebook. The act of reading seemed gently to change her. She no longer stuck out one skinny hip or did unconscious things with her toes. Her voice was unaffected, pleasant to listen to, and only a few of the words gave her any trouble. As she read, a softness drifted over her like a veil. She looked young and promising and possibly lovely, like a girl her own age, like the girls at Beatrice's school. She could easily have been one of them: on the verge of something, brimming. With what, it had yet to be revealed, but still there it was, that fullness. As she read, it appeared very possible that she wouldn't be stuck forever behind the scenery, or pursing her lips above a flute, or folding the guest towels with fastidious content. As she read the words carefully from her notebook, her sister, listening, felt that there was hope.

Maggie looked up and smiled; the last sentence hung charmingly in the air. Beatrice beamed at her from the end of the table. By now their mother had paused in her chopping and was studying them both.

"That essay," she said, "was about a musical."

"Yes," said Maggie, closing her notebook. "*Cats.*"

"But the play you did was *The Caucasian Chalk Circle.*"

"I know," said Maggie. "But *Cats* just seemed to fit better."

"Did you notice the parallels she made?" asked Beatrice. "Between the kids who work backstage and all the characters in the play? Each with their own funny quirks and personality!"

Their mother ignored her. She looked steadily at Maggie. "You haven't even seen *Cats.*"

"Beatrice told me the whole story. She sang some parts from the songs." Maggie opened up her notebook again, uncertainly. "You didn't like it?"

"I'm not saying I didn't like it."

"You have to admit, this version is much stronger than the other one," Beatrice said.

Her mother turned to her. "You were in *Cats.*"

"It's called creative nonfiction!" Beatrice cried. She glanced over at her sister, who was silently rereading the pages with a puckered, doubtful expression. "This is a better essay, believe me."

"I don't care if it's better," their mother declared, and went back to her cleaver and cutting board and the eviscerated bell peppers. "We'll keep working on it," she said over her shoulder to Maggie, and then to Beatrice, now standing beside her, "Is this how you help your students at school?"

The question was real, which made it far worse than if it were merely mean. It was all Beatrice could do to keep from throwing herself beneath her mother's rat-a-tat knife, moving at lightning speed across the board. She was only trying to give Maggie an edge, an advantage—didn't they understand the urgency? She knew, better than they, what the competition actually looked like. But the two of them seemed determined to proceed innocently, undaunted. Outside in the cold, as Maggie calculated her profits, their mother had mentioned that the high school offered a Young Entrepreneurs Club (Beatrice had asked, Is that like a Young Republicans Club?), then Maggie had chimed in that she could take classes in Mandarin, too. Who needed an ancient, rolling campus? Beatrice realized with a pang that they were busy making the best of things, something that she, so accustomed to the best, had never quite learned how to do.

"Sorry," she murmured.

She stole a sliver of green pepper; she ran her fingers along the edge of the kitchen table, unearthing her student's homemade birthday card from beneath the newspaper. On it was a picture of a stick-figure girl with a bubble head and a tiny red mouth—out of her mouth issued a yellow balloon containing the words: *Today Is Great!*—and inside the card the yellow balloon continued, explaining: *Great Because YOU Were Born! (with a smile!)* The exclamation marks all carried hearts instead of dots. Standing there, her fingers resting lightly on its surface, Beatrice found herself fighting the urge to open this card, but in the end she lost.

THAT NIGHT SHE RETREATED to her former bedroom, where she sniffed the comforter warily and wondered who else might be sleeping there in months to come. Near eleven Maggie appeared in the doorway with a Ouija board as an offering. "The directions say that you're supposed to do this with two people." She climbed up onto the foot of the bed. "A lady and a gentleman preferred, it says, but I think it'll still work if it's two ladies."

Beatrice put down her book. "You've really never done this before?"

"In fifth grade Evie Rosenthal came face to face with pure evil," said Maggie.

She was wearing a faded sweatshirt and a pair of thermal underwear. She didn't look especially prepared to welcome messengers from the spirit world. Whatever happened to cute pajamas? Beatrice wondered. She thought back sadly on all her little nightgowns, the flowers, the bits of eyelet, the ruffled hems. Even when she turned punk rock she wore pretty things to bed, things sent to her by her grandmothers. But Maggie had no grandmothers—they were all gone, exiting in quick succession by the time she was four.

"Who are you trying to contact?" Beatrice asked. She saw her Po-Po and her Nana and her Grandma Sara standing there expectantly on the other side, their feeble arms full of red Macy's boxes with nightgowns tucked into tissue paper. It would be nice to talk to them. They looked as if they wanted to say something kind.

"Oh. I didn't know you had to pick someone in particular. I just have a few general questions I need answered." Maggie unfolded the board, and Beatrice, by the water stain in the corner, recognized it as her own. Her father would forget to go down to the basement and empty the dehumidifier. "Can we do that? Just ask the universe? We don't want to bother anyone."

"Sure. Why not. We'll ask the all-purpose universe," Beatrice said, though this seemed the supernatural equivalent of worshipping at a Unitarian church, with sofas instead of pews, and not a cross in sight. "What are we asking?"

"Just a few business-related things," said Maggie. "You

should think up some questions, too. That way we can take turns."

"I wouldn't even know where to begin. We'd be here all night."

"I don't mind. Tomorrow's Sunday."

"I'm tired, Maggie."

"I know!" She gave a little bounce at the end of the bed. "You can ask who your next fiancé is going to be!"

Beatrice smiled. That was sweet. She liked how it sounded, as if she were a restless beauty with husbands and broken hearts trailing in her wake, and not a seventh-grade English teacher of dubious judgment and middling abilities whose brief and lucky engagement had ended, and who was now alone. Today was her birthday; today she turned twenty-nine years old.

Whoosh! From out of nowhere, the sheer force of self-pity. She rose sputtering to the surface, soggy and blinded.

"Should we turn off the lights?" Maggie asked.

They lit a candle so they could see. It was shaped like a little seashell and perhaps had come packaged with the soaps. The board shone dully between them, waiting to begin the conversation. Despite herself, Beatrice felt an old flutter of excitement. She had once been an avid practitioner. They would all go down to the basement and allow strange things to occur. She and her friends from school, when they were the same age as Maggie. They rigged towels over the tiny basement window to make the room even darker, and they sat on the cold floor in a circle, and stopped breathing, and the little plastic contraption would go skating wildly across the board. Beatrice liked to speak with the sad ghost of Marilyn Monroe, who said yes to almost every question she was asked. Will it happen? Does he like me? Can I have it? When she said no, it was bad. Someone else had come on the line. Someone angry. Beneath their fingertips, someone tugging. A burnt smell. An electric buzzing in the air. I—AM—SA—They jerked away their hands in fear. They scrambled back from the board, unable to speak, hearts beating fast. They couldn't look at each other. They couldn't move. What had they done? What door had they opened? The terror of television static, the scratching of a needle caught in the final groove. Turn it off, fast! That feeling. But they couldn't move. The door was open. The sound of footsteps on the stairs. Clomp. Clomp. The towel falling from the window with a whump, but no light coming in. The darkness even darker. The footsteps heavy and close. Clomp. Clomp. Hearts racing, lungs panting. Clomp. Clomp. And then—

A big Dracula laugh.

Mwahh-haaa-haaa-haaaaaaa.

"Papa!" she screamed. He came staggering into the basement. His glasses glowed dimly. He held his arms up in the air, as if about to descend on them with a billowing black cape. But he was wearing a tie and sport coat instead. A dank hiccup escaped from the dehumidifier.

Her friends collapsed on each other, shrieking. She let out her breath and folded her arms around him.

"Are your eyes closed?" Maggie asked. "Are you relaxed?"

"Yes," Beatrice said. She felt everything inside her slowly coming loose.

Her hands joined her sister's on the contraption. The candle was making the whole room smell like cake. How good it felt to rest her eyes, to rest her fingers on the plastic, to let the unseen forces take over for a little while. She tried to conjure up a picture of the universe and saw Styrofoam balls of varying sizes gently bobbing in the breeze. No. That was the solar system, abandoned weeks ago in her homeroom after the science fair. The universe was bigger, much bigger. She would have to try harder.

"I'm asking my question now," Maggie whispered.

"Go for it."

"I'm asking it silently, actually. I'm asking it in my head."

"Then what am I supposed to do?" Beatrice opened her eyes a crack. "The whole point is to be collaborative."

Maggie sighed, her eyes still closed. "Well. Just think of Mama. Think of Mama and me on a beach in the Caribbean."

"Doing tai chi?"

"Okay. If you want." She paused. "Think Aruba."

That was easy. She could handle Aruba. White sand. Turquoise water. A scattering of cabanas. Beatrice squeezed her eyes shut and drifted over the island. She saw two little figures standing in the surf. Above her the black wind of the galaxies swept by. A passing comet showered her in sparkles. To her surprise, she was turning. And somewhere far away, her hands began to move. She tumbled through the ether like a satellite, keeping one eye fixed on the island below. White sand. Blue-green water. Her hands slid away from her. Which way was Yes? Which way was No? She couldn't remember. She couldn't remember if the board was upside-down or not. All she could do was watch the two people circling in slow motion at the edge of the sea. What was it that her sister wanted? An offshore bank account. A Princess cruise. Waves crashed, moons pulled, planets spun. Black holes swallowed everything in sight. The beautiful universe went on and on. I don't care what she wants, Beatrice thought as her hands traveled below her and she, slowly tumbling, beamed her message into space:

Marilyn?

Papa?

Say yes.

Bump

Many years later, she was on her way to see some trees. A magnificent London plane tree, more than sixty-three inches in diameter, and an allée of horse chestnuts, somewhat sickly and tattered but still of interest. Of interest to her, who now spent her days thinking about such things. Gradation, drainage, compacted soil. Canopy coverage. The secret lives of city trees. They grew shadily at the perimeters of her imagination, and along the blocks she now walked to the park entrance from the station. Beautiful and various and unavoidable, trees: and yet working in the urban forest she still found great wide-open spaces in her mind where no trees grew at all. On this day, for instance, as she walked from the station to the park in a neighborhood she had no reason to visit, except for the horse chestnuts, she was thinking about something else entirely.

A girl with a wonderful butt was walking a few feet ahead of her. She didn't even know how to assemble the phrase in her head—ass? bottom? There was no comfortable way of describing it. But seeing the girl from behind made her happy. She had first noticed her climbing the stairs from the station—her white flip-flops looking improbably clean against the grimy, gummed-up steps. Neat little ankles, lean calves. A cheap silky skirt—also white, with orange swirls—that ended just at the back of her knee. All of this moving crisply up the dirty stairs, as deliciously as a new pair of scissors biting into a sheet of paper. At the top the girl turned left and crossed over to the bright side of the street. In a stroke of fortune, she was headed toward the park. There were four whole blocks in which to wonder at her high, brisk bottom and the charming way it undulated beneath the thin material of her skirt.

Undulate? Oh, help us. The word was practically dripping with oily intent. It really was impossible to walk behind a girl with a pretty butt—in objective appreciation—and not sound hopelessly slimy, even to oneself.

But a pregnant woman couldn't be slimy. She might be constipated or gassy or luminous, but not slimy. And in her case, she was pregnant, objectively pregnant. If she found herself studying girls on the subway and the street, her gaze was not envious—she had never had neat ankles to begin with—but acquisitive. Collecting traits for the small body she was, to her deep bemusement, cultivating. She wanted nail beds that were long and narrow, shoulder blades that flared like wings. She liked freckles, back dimples, feet with nice arches. On her way to see some significant trees, she was walking behind a girl and thinking, I hope its butt will look just like that.

The girl turned around.

"Ms. Hempel?"

It had been ages since anyone called her that.

"Sophie?" she asked, shocked that the person she'd been following was in fact a familiar one. Hard to imagine that this blithe creature was once stuck in the seventh grade. Sophie Lohmann. She would never forget their names, even years and years later; they were carved roughly and indelibly somewhere. "Oh, Sophie! Look at you."

The young woman—she was not a girl anymore—smiled and retraced her steps. She held out her lovely arms for a hug.

"How are you? What's going on? Tell me everything!" said Ms. Hempel, laughing joyfully and nervously, awash in Sophie's lollipop perfume, surprised that even as grown-ups her girls still offered the same diffident, bony embraces as they did when they were children.

And how unexpected that Sophie Lohmann, of all those girls, should excite in her this rush of affection! Sophie with her unsettling doll-tiny features and huge kewpie eyes, now smoky with makeup. Not a soul that Ms. Hempel thought about much anymore, though at the time she had made enough of an impression. Sophie was new to the school, a new girl then. In the first few days she gave an elaborate performance of shyness and hesitancy that was later revealed to be purely perfunctory. She knew she'd be fine. How could she not be? She was cute and thin and blond and clever. Universal currency, accepted everywhere. But there was something in the pertness of her looks, or maybe it was her manner, that struck Ms. Hempel as uncanny, antiquated, as if Sophie were a re-suscitated bobby-soxer with a little bit of freezer burn around the edges. On some days she would even take a curling iron to her ponytail. "Good morning, Ms. Hempel!" she'd say with a surplus of sweetness that made her blond ringlets bounce crazily about.

All that simpering—she never faltered. And she never once let her spine droop; she never slouched. Having abandoned her ballet career, she still kept a strict eye on her posture. During all-school assemblies, Ms. Hempel always knew where Sophie was sitting: the one child perfectly erect among the bodies hunched on the gymnasium floor. What else? What else came floating up out of the strange, drifting sediment? The sugary

perfume made her dizzy. She couldn't remember a lick of Sophie's schoolwork—though maybe she did fancy covers for her
book reports. There was a younger brother, in the fifth grade,
who had starred in a peanut-butter commercial. A free trip
to Hawaii, thanks to a magazine contest the mother had won
with a photo essay about her kitchen renovation. Ms. Hempel
couldn't remember ever meeting this mother, or the father for
that matter; she had no recollection of them at all. Which only
heightened her sense of Sophie's slightly concocted quality.
What else. What else? Nothing more came to mind, except of
course the fear: the embarrassing feeling of fear this girl had
kindled in her.

"It's so weird," Sophie was saying. "I was just talking about
that Constitution thing we did. Remember? When we went to
that big courthouse downtown and everybody dressed up in
jackets and ties? And we pretended to be lawyers in the Supreme Court? I was a justice; I wore a choir robe you got from
Mrs. Willoughby. I think you gave me a B on the decision I
wrote, which I didn't quite understand, seeing that I worked
really hard on it. But this is the important part: the whole case
was about anthrax! Do remember that?"

"I do," said Ms. Hempel, nodding rapidly, already mar-
shaling silent arguments in defense of the ancient B. "I remember all of it."

"So don't you think that's weird? Here we were, talking
theoretically about anthrax. I didn't even know what it was
before then—"

To be honest, neither had Ms. Hempel. She thought Anthrax was a band who played their guitars demonically fast.
But thankfully the Constitution unit came equipped with an
instructor's guide, which out of vanity she kept hidden inside
a bland and unincriminating notebook.

"But we became experts on it! We spent a month talking about nothing but anthrax. That little island they infected during World War Two, and then in Russia when it got out by accident and killed so many people and they covered it up."

"We also talked about the Pentagon Papers. We talked a lot about those," Ms. Hempel pointed out, as if for the benefit of a parent standing nearby. "And other relevant cases. Precedents . . ." She couldn't summon up any of them by name, the teacher's guide long lost by now. But look what surfaced from the murky depths! The red plastic binding, the jaunty little logo with the flag. Sophie's appearance had really set things astir. "National security versus freedom of speech," Ms. Hempel said triumphantly, reading the heavy block letters on the title page. "That's what we were talking about."

"I guess so. But what I remember most was the anthrax," Sophie said, and glanced down at her opalescent toenails, which wiggled back at her from the flawless white flip-flops. "And that's why I completely freaked out. You know, when it really happened. The letters with the spores, and people dying. I knew everything already, everything they were talking about on the news." She lifted her huge smoky eyes to Ms. Hempel. "And I know this sounds crazy, but the whole thing felt psychic. Or maybe prophetic. I had this feeling that we had made it happen somehow, by getting dressed up and taking it so seriously, going to that courtroom and pretending like it was real. Not like it was our fault, exactly, but more like it was something we had brought into the world by talking about it so much."

She laughed suddenly, a pretty sound.

"So I was telling this to my friend the other night, and he says that either I'm paranoid or a total narcissist. He's still trying to figure it out."

Sophie couldn't help smiling slightly to herself at the mention of this unnamed friend, this friend who was contemplating her personality disorders. Ms. Hempel knew that happy, inward look. That buzzy feeling. And she knew that if Sophie was gazing so softly and fondly at her now, on this sunny, dirty block lined with its malodorous ginkgo trees, it was only because Sophie had spoken of her to this friend, and that she and anthrax and the United States Constitution had all been graced, made golden, by his skeptical attention.

"But seriously," said Sophie. "Didn't that freak you out?"

Well, yes, it freaked her out. Sure it did. It freaked her out to remember that the most terrible things in the world had once been her handy tools for the sharpening of critical-thinking skills, the assigning of argumentative essays, the fostering of middle school debate. Frequent visitors in her classroom, the theoretical terrorists—they dropped in all the time. Her innocence (stupidity?) was astounding. About everything— dangers outside and in. To think that she once found Travis Bent's misanthropy endearing! His gloomy looks, his jittering leg, his bloody works of fiction. Now she'd have to report him. When he was put on medication, he took to signing his name as "Travis Bent, 50 mg"—and she thought it droll. But everything had changed. A kid couldn't be left to his own odd and unsociable ways; a teacher couldn't call upon the phantom terrorists to illustrate a point. The delicate, treacherous scrim was torn. Three parents from her school had been lost. And what an oblivious twit she'd been for all those years, leading her little ducks on picnic outings along the brink of the abyss. From the great distance of her thirties, she peered down and saw the tiny figures playing kick ball while behind them opened up an immense and roiling pit of darkness. It made her sweat, that picture in her head. Then again, a certain well-scrubbed sort of blue autumn morning gave her pause, too. What was she doing, procreating? Looking at trees? What in the world was she doing. . . .

Before her stood Sophie Lohmann, survivor: of the seventh grade, of Ms. Hempel's innocence, of the hazardous times that had befallen everyone since then. Sophie, searching through a dainty handbag for her phone. Standing there pristinely on the sidewalk, she looked indestructible and full of secrets. The phone kept humming, humming, humming until she pinched it savagely and it stopped. The little strap was hoisted back up onto her shoulder, the purse tucked beneath her armpit like a football. Its color was pale orange, like the swirling patterns in her skirt.

"Sorry about that," said Sophie, frowning. It wasn't her friend who had called; someone else. She swept back her hair, shaking off an invisible dusting of filth. "So, Ms. Hempel," she said seriously. "You're done with graduate school? You're teaching college now?"

Ms. Hempel hesitated, half pleased and half chagrined. For how kind it was of them, her former students, to remember these things, to keep track of her muddled goals and aspirations! "No, no. Not at all. I sort of changed direction." And how complicated it was for her to explain where she happened to find herself now. "The program wasn't really what I'd expected. We didn't spend a lot of time reading actual novels." Just slim little volumes of theory—and not of the congenial French variety—as well as religious pamphlets, etiquette manuals, ship manifests, broadsides, classified advertisements. Who knew that the definition of literary text had become quite so all-encompassing? It was her own fault.

When Mr. Polidori left the science department to earn his master's in—of all beautiful things—music composition, she had thought, *Aha!* School would save her. A noble exit, provided by her lifelong commitment to learning. She made a dash for the escape hatch. "And I was a redundancy. Nobody wants to see another dissertation about the Brontë sisters or the Shakespeare romance plays or *Tess of the D'Urbervilles.*"

"That's terrible!" cried Sophie. "I love Shakespeare."

"I'm a dropout!" Ms. Hempel announced good-naturedly.

Sophie found this perturbing. Her eyebrows twitched. "Do you think they'll let you back in?"

"I found something else to do," said Ms. Hempel hazily, reluctant to trudge up her unlikely path again: the temporary job that turned without warning into a real job, the classes at night, the slow acquiring of a new vocabulary, not to mention an entirely new way of seeing. "I don't want to go back. You shouldn't look so worried. It's something I love." She then said the words that usually cheered people up: Planning. Conservation. Design. But Sophie's tiny eyebrows refused to relax.

"Good for you," she said finally.

"I'm on my way to the park. Isn't that where you're heading?"

"I live here, Ms. Hempel," said Sophie with dignity, nodding at the long glowing row of brick fronts and brownstones, worn and well loved, in uneven states of repair. "I'm just coming home." Oh yes; Ms. Hempel remembered. A flushed, tearful discussion in English class—what were they reading, *The House on Mango Street?*—about good neighborhoods and bad. But Sophie had nothing to be ashamed of now: There was a wine shop! And a sushi place. A store devoted to baby clothes made of organic cotton. Her maligned corner of the world—

just look at it now. And Sophie herself had been the harbinger of all this.

"So it's your park! How lucky you are," Ms. Hempel said. "You must know it inside and out."

"I don't think I'd be much help," Sophie said, misunderstanding. "It's not like I hang out there. I don't have a dog or anything. I mean, we go there sometimes, but only when . . ." She trailed off suggestively, then offered a little grin.

"Oh please," Ms. Hempel said. "I'm not your teacher anymore." And the two of them tried to laugh.

But herein lay their problem, precisely—if she wasn't Sophie's teacher, then who was she? And who was Sophie now, if not a bright-eyed seventh grader? A girl in too much makeup, a girl with a perfect behind. A girl who was taking an undetermined amount of time off from college and manning the front desk of a health club, where she offered up towels to busy people in ties (and the teacher felt a sure prick of disappointment upon hearing this). But they couldn't let each other go; they couldn't pass with just a startled wave and a smile. Though that would have been the gentler way! Instead of all the anxious pawing, the sniffing around, as each tried to dig up what was dearly buried in the other.

Ms. Hempel wished she could summon up the old, fearful, Sophie feeling. That slight tightening in her stomach, as if at the sound of a distant alarm, an invisible trip wire set off by the batting of Sophie's eyelashes or the rolling of her enormous eyes. The fluttering eyelashes were on display all the time; but the eye-rolling she would catch only fleetingly, on rare occasions, just as she was turning back to the blackboard or ushering her class out the door. Those tricky looks! They made Ms. Hempel afraid. As if Sophie's coyness and fawning were merely her flimsy disguise for a violent, barely controlled contempt. At any moment this derision might be unleashed—and her teacher would be dead meat. Her drooping tights; her hysterical hand gestures; her insistence that everyone, everyone, finish their outlines by Friday! In other words, Ms. Hempel was just begging to be laid out, flattened—no, obliterated—by Sophie's rolling eyeballs. Remember you're the grown-up, Ms. Hempel would reason. All the power is yours. You give out detention, you give out grades, bathroom passes, chocolate bars—you're in charge! While she, she's only a child.

Monologues that were of little help or solace.

True, Sophie was a child; but she was also a person, a young one but a definite person nonetheless. This was the feeling that Ms. Hempel couldn't shake: a conviction that she spent her days among people at the age when they were most purely themselves. How could she not be depleted when she came home, having been exposed for hours, without protection, to all of those thrumming, radiant selves? Here they were, just old enough to have discovered their souls, but not yet dulled by the ordinary act of survival, not yet practiced at dissembling. Even Sophie, consummate performer, was as transparent as glass. The terror, the thrill, of encountering such superiority in its undiluted form! Those baby-doll eyes just shimmering with scorn. Ms. Hempel was regularly undone. But any other encounter proved no less shattering: in Cilla Matsui, with sympathy; in Emily Radinsky, with genius; in Jonathan Hamish, with wildness and beauty and torment.

"Does this mean I can call you Beatrice now?" Sophie asked, and Beatrice said yes, thus ending the search. The dimpling and disdainful child—the person—was nowhere to be found. This clean young woman was standing in her place.

"Finally! Beatrice. It's funny, because I always kind of thought we should call you that, and now that I can, it sounds completely strange."

"You thought of me as a kid?" Beatrice asked, brushing off some bagel crumbs that had found their way to the front of her shirt. "Inexperienced, maybe? Or just lacking authority?"

And as much as it might have sounded like a question she would have asked in her past—a question frankly in search of assurances or compliments—she was asking it now because she was simply interested, and felt nothing but a cool curiosity, as if she were inquiring about a person quite separate from herself.

"No," said Sophie, "you were like a real teacher. That wasn't why." She paused to think. "I guess I felt that way because we were close to you."

Beatrice looked up, stunned by this kindness, but Sophie appeared to have taken no notice of it.

"I don't know why I even asked. As if I could ever get used to calling you anything but Ms. Hempel. That's ironic, isn't it? We still think of you as Ms. Hempel and we're almost the same age you were when you started teaching us."

Could that be possible? Was she really that young? Of course, at the time she had felt washed up, nearly ruined. Her first birthday in the faculty lunchroom: staring dolefully at a little tub of rice pudding and sighing, "I can't believe I'm turning the big two-four," and Mrs. Willoughby, upon hearing this, hooting with laughter.

"Not quite the same age," Beatrice said. "In a few more years."

"Well, close enough. We'll be there soon. The point is I was over at Jonathan's and we were all sitting around talking—"

"Jonathan?" Beatrice said. "Jonathan Hamish?"

"I know. Weird. There's sort of a group of us—Eli, Roderick, Julia Rizzo—how random is that? And Robert Levy-Cohen. He goes by Bob now. Remember how quiet he used to be all the time? Well, it turns out he's crazy. Completely hilarious . . ." Sophie smiled to herself, and began drifting once again toward that dark, blank space that Beatrice realized she did not in any way wish to see further illuminated. Whatever they were up to in their newfound adulthood, she did not want to know. The dusky parks, the shifting neighborhoods, the old bedrooms and kitchens, emptied of parents. . . . She found herself wrapping her cardigan more tightly around her in some sort of feeble precautionary measure. Meanwhile, Sophie made her way back to the bright sidewalk. "You know, when everyone graduated, it was like we couldn't wait to get out of there, to meet actual new people. But then after the first year or so, the first few years, we all started coming home and hanging out again. It's not as pathetic as it sounds. Did you know that his mom got remarried? Jonathan's. Their place is huge."

When was the last time she had laid eyes on Jonathan Hamish? Years and years ago, as he was being carted away by the police. No, she shouldn't even think that, not even jokingly. But that was the look he had about him—slouching, defiant, richly amused—as Mr. Peele escorted him back inside the school building. He'd been causing trouble in the courtyard.

Eighth period, American history. Whap! Whap! The sharp sound of cracking, of something possibly being broken. Ms. Hempel wheeled around from the blackboard and glared. "Brad . . . ," she said ominously, and the boy held up his hands with the indignation of someone who for the first time in his life has been wrongly accused. The class was gazing at the window, the one next to the dusty air conditioner, and Lila put down her pencil and pointed. "It's coming from out there."

Ms. Hempel went to investigate. Whap! She flinched. The window shuddered. Down in the courtyard, the varsity track team were milling about as they waited to board the school bus, fuming at the curb, that would deliver them to some far-away campus for their meet. Draped in their glossy warm-up suits, the boys loped elegantly about the yard, their long bodies leaning to one side, weighted down by their voluminous gym bags. Some were pulling cans from the soda machine, others stretching themselves across the steps. Occupied and blameless, as far as she could tell. Then, whap! A face squinted up at her from below. A hand hung suspended in the air.

She slid the glass open. "Jonathan?"

He gave her a lopsided smile. "Hi."

"Enough with the window-breaking," she said. "We're trying to do manifest destiny up here."

He looked at her blankly.

"Cut it out, okay? It's dangerous." She was too far away to see what was happening in his eyes. "Okay?"

She drew back into the room and tugged down the sash.

No sooner had she closed it: Whap! The class, hunched forward in their desk-chairs, ecstatic with the distraction, let out a breathless little laugh. Whap!

"Jonathan," she sighed, and reopened the window.

She saw that he had an endless supply: the pool of gray pebbles out of which a sad, spindly tree had been trying for ages to grow. Jonathan's one hand was cupped, heavy with ammunition, while his other hand had found the deep pocket of his tracksuit.

She gazed down at him. "What."

"Is it true that you're leaving?"

"Are you serious?"

He shrugged. "I was wondering. I just wanted to know."

"And it couldn't wait."

"So it's true, then. You're leaving." With a softly spilling sound, he released his handful of pebbles back into their small enclosure. Then he glanced up, as if struck by a sudden thought. "You shouldn't leave," he said.

"I'm going back to school."

"School?" he asked, incredulous. "What for?"

"I'm not going to yell it out the window!" She could hear the happiness in her own voice. "Couldn't you have asked me in the hallway? Or some other place where people have conversations?"

But he wasn't even looking at her anymore. His attention had already roamed elsewhere, and here she was leaning halfway out the window, hollering. She straightened at once, hands back on the sash, and as she declared, "I'm trying to teach right now," she saw the mass of bodies in the courtyard part neatly along the middle, and Mr. Peele come bearing down on him.

He would be missing his meet that afternoon. And if he was still anything like he used to be in the eighth grade, she knew this was the one punishment that mattered, that devastated him. Absurdly, she felt the fault was hers. And though she was certain there must have been other sightings before the year ended, this was the last time she could actually remember seeing him—his brave, shuffling walk up the steps in the shadow of tall Mr. Peele.

"So the man his mom married," Sophie continued, "makes bank. He started a company and then he sold it. Technically I should call him Jonathan's stepdad, but seeing that he came kind of late into the picture, it doesn't seem like there's a whole lot of parenting left to be done. So we just call him Jeff. Or sometimes *Jefe*, but really only Bob calls him that." Beatrice felt grateful as she half listened to Sophie's sweet and inscrutable chatter, grateful that Sophie was the stranger she happened to be following from the station, and not another child, not Jonathan, for instance. "Jeff's very interested in technology," said Sophie, "and he subscribes to all of those magazines, and they've turned the whole garden level into—his word—a media center. It's completely gorgeous. It's like being inside a movie theater. But he won't let you go down there holding even so much as a soda. Can you believe that? It's criminal: an entire media center gone to waste. So we're stuck up in Jonathan's room, everybody trying to fit on his bed, and there's nothing to do except watch the guys play *Grand Theft Auto* on the little beat-up TV that used to be in his old house."

"That is criminal," Beatrice murmured.

"Julia will play sometimes, but I can't stand it—those games make me sick. They give me headaches. So I have to entertain myself. And the other night, I'm poking around and looking at all these pictures he has taped up on the door of his closet—and I shriek, literally, because there is a photo of Bessie Blustein!" Oh, Bessie Blustein—Beatrice winced—that tortured soul whose name was as wrongly bovine and placid as her appearance. She had left the school after the eighth grade to reinvent herself as a gothic Elizabeth. "It was a picture from that day at the courthouse—she was wearing her choir robe, too. And whoever said that black is slimming . . . well, they never saw Bessie Blustein dressed up as a Supreme Court justice. I know, that's really mean of me. I bet she's lost a lot of weight by now. But in the picture she's this big black smudge in the middle. To be fair, the photograph is pretty blurry. And I say to Jonathan, 'What are you doing with a picture of Bessie Blustein on your wall?' and he says, without even looking up from the game: fuck Bessie Blustein, it's a picture of *you*. Meaning you, Ms. Hempel. And he says it with this voice like, you idiot. Meaning me. So I look more closely, and sure enough, there you are! Up in the corner, way in the background, trying to fix Ben Vrabel's tie."

A slow warmth suffused Beatrice's face, her body—she felt as if she'd been set alight.

"And that's when we started talking about the whole Constitution thing we did. Which is why it was still on my mind when I was talking to my friend. Don't worry, you don't know him, he didn't go to our school. But here's what I was trying to say: we still called you Ms. Hempel! We sounded like a bunch of little kids. Right in middle of a serious discussion about the war, presidential powers, civil liberties, all that stuff. Completely incongruous. But that's what I mean: you're Ms. Hempel forever. At least to us. "

Beatrice was smiling uncontrollably.

"I know! Incongruous. You taught us that word," Sophie said. "I still use it all the time. That, and *precarious*."

Beatrice didn't know what to do with herself, with this ridiculous feeling of joy, so she threw her arms around Sophie for another hug. "That's about the nicest thing anyone has ever told me," she said into a curtain of slippery hair. All she wanted to do now was float away, or at least travel the remaining two blocks to the park where in the shade of its enormous plane tree she could unwrap the story and gaze at it quietly by herself. What a reversal—usually it was the young person itching to get away from the old—and here was puffy, aching Beatrice, making polite excuses to the most beautiful of girls.

"I need to pop into the store, anyhow," said Sophie, untucking her orange purse. "I know, don't give me that look; I know that it's a disgusting habit. But it's mine now!" she said cheerfully as she pulled an almost-empty pack of cigarettes from her bag.

"Kisses," she cried, and stepped away, while Beatrice panicked, not knowing what she could give in return.

"You look breathtaking, Sophie!" she called. "Did I tell you that? You look glorious. All the way from the station I was walking behind you and thinking, what a beautiful, beautiful person . . ."

"Oh. Thanks," Sophie said vaguely, as though she'd received this tribute so many times that it had ceased to mean anything at all. "That's really sweet."

Now it appeared as if she were the one who suddenly longed to get away.

"And I meant to ask," persisted Beatrice, "whatever made you turn around? Because I'm so glad you did. Otherwise I never would have realized it was you, and we never would have had this chance to talk. But isn't that an unusual thing? I almost wondered if you could hear what I was thinking. Because that's odd, isn't it—to just turn around as you're walking down the street?"

A short, brittle laugh burst out of Sophie. "I'm not going to bore you with the long version, but needless to say, there's a guy involved." Famously, she rolled her eyes; but this time there was more than just contempt in the gesture, there was also weariness, and maybe something else. "Put it this way: it's my new habit. Being aware of my surroundings. You know what I mean?"

Oh yes, fear. That's what it was. Beatrice weakly held up

her hand in a wave. "Well, be careful," she said pointlessly. She pulled her sweater closer as she watched Sophie disappear inside the grubby store.

The two blocks that separated her from the park now struck her as an impossible distance. This happened more and more often, the abrupt onslaught of exhaustion. If she were to sink right down onto one of those worn stoops, would they let her stay? She realized she hadn't even told Sophie—who probably just assumed she'd grown fat. And she didn't remember to mention that she had a new name. No one, not even the solicitors who bothered her on the phone, called her Ms. Hempel anymore. And other new names were likely to come, among them Mama, most strangely. Or Mom. Something her students would on a rare occasion call her when they were deeply lost in concentration—an accident, of course, and they would blush.

SHE HAD BEEN HAVING SUCH DREAMS—a common phenomenon, said the books—but how could dreams like these be considered in any way common? She'd wake up late in the morning, throbbing with surprise and pleasure, aghast at what her subconscious was capable of. It seemed a good argument for sleeping even more than she already was. And that particular night, as might be expected, she dreamt once again of school, not one of the fretful dreams that used to dog her even long after she had stopped teaching, but a gentle dream, a beautiful dream. When she woke, her face was wet, and there was only one fragment she could remember: the long hallway outside her classroom, and the eerie light coming through the mottled glass of the doors that swung at the end of the hall, and the feeling of moving down the passageway very slowly and deliberately. There was someone beside her, also moving. A child—no taller than her shoulder, half a step behind, breathing hoarsely—whom she loved. Together they were walking down the hallway, headed toward some bright, severe place where they didn't really want to go. It was her role to take the child there and then return; she could hear the muffled roar of her classroom at their backs, and all the kids stirring around inside, waiting. But for now she was alone with the child she loved, walking farther down the hall, deeper into the silence, the strange glow ahead of them, the child slipping his hand into hers and she holding it lightly, the whole dream filling with her wish that their steps would grow slower, and the passage grow longer, so that they might never have to reach the place where they were supposed to arrive.